Mr. Wrong

Mr. Wrong

Terry Campbell

Five Star
Unity, Maine

This novel is a work of fiction. Names, characters, places, and incidents are either the product of the author's imagination, or, if real, used fictitiously.

Five Star First Edition Romance.
Published in conjunction with Linda D. Campbell &
Bobbye R. Terry.

Five Star Standard Print First Edition Romance Series.

The text of this edition is unabridged.

Set in 11 pt. Plantin by Al Chase.

Printed in the United States on permanent paper.

Library of Congress Cataloging-in-Publication Data
Campbell, Terry.
    Mr. Wrong / by Terry Campbell.
      p.   cm.
    ISBN 0-7862-2154-2 (hc : alk. paper)
    I. Title.
  PS3553.A48744M7 1999
  813'.54—dc21

                                                    99-38418

Mr. Wrong

CHAPTER ONE

She'd baited the trap with a home-cooked meal and sprang it over dessert. Damn! This woman wasn't the Kat he'd known since childhood. Nor was she the logical, bottom-line thinking CPA of his law firm. This Kat Snow was an unknown quantity. She had an agenda, and he was it.

Rourke Hawthorne's hand tightened on the ivory lined sheet of paper.

Mr. Right

1. *Likes children. Must pass the Tory test.*
2. *Genuinely likes women.*
3. *Doesn't want just sex, but a grandé passion!*
4. *Tall. At least six feet.*
5. *Eye color—blue, brown, green, or hazel. NO GRAY.*
6. *Good looking—handsome isn't a prerequisite. Nice body, broad shoulders, narrow hips welcomed.*
7. *Sense of humor.*
8. *Not threatened by my job or independence.*
9. *A professional. Can't be autocratic, dictatorial, or controlling.*

Hiding behind the neutral facade he wore in court, Rourke lifted his gaze. "Hmm, Kat—"

"I know I shouldn't ask, but I need your help."

Help? With what? Marriage? With the exception of number five, her list fit him as perfectly as his favorite baseball mitt. Rourke leaned back in the chair.

How could he let her down easy? Dissuade her of this insane idea that he was Mr. Right? Let's see. Certainly, he could be diplomatic. Of course he could; he was a lawyer. He'd say—

"I need your help in preparing to re-enter the meat market and finding the one gentleman left in Northern Virginia."

Rourke's chair crashed forward. "Meat market? But . . . This is . . . I . . ."

"You didn't think . . . Oh, my!" Kat laughed. "You aren't what I'm looking for, Rourke. You don't meet my criteria."

"What am I? Mr. Wrong?" *Get a grip, man. This is your out.* "Kat—"

"I didn't mean to hurt your pride."

"You didn't. Why doesn't the list fit me?"

"I never took you for a masochist."

Rourke glared at her. Masochist, like hell. If the glove fit, wear it. He retrieved the list and shook his head. "One look at this list confirms the truth. Except for my gray eyes, I'm a perfect match."

"Oh, please." Kat scooted to his side of the kitchen table. She pointed to number one. "See this? It says likes children. You once told me the only good child was medium rare."

Rourke shifted in his chair. "I've never felt like that about Tory, only those screaming rug rats in stores."

"Whatever. I still can't see you with a baby, feedings, or dirty diapers."

"That's a low blow, Kat."

"Hey, I'm not the one who tossed his cookies when his niece needed her dirty diaper changed."

"I'd just worked out and it was over ninety," Rourke muttered as she snickered beside him. "What about number two? I like women."

8

He winced at the gentle pat on his arm and braced himself. Something told him she remembered every throwaway line he'd ever uttered and they were all about to come back and bite him in the butt.

"When I was fourteen you said women were made for three things; to make love, make babies, and make a man's life hell. Doesn't sound like genuine *like* to me."

Yup, he'd felt the crunch. "For God's sake, Kat, I was only twenty-one!"

Kat shrugged. "You haven't changed that much."

He had everything else knocked. It was a home run. He could see the ball flying out of the park. "You can't argue with my being tall, I'm six feet. Most women think I'm good looking and a great lover."

He winced at the pity in her eyes and the negative shake of her head.

"Number three says no casual sex. While you *enjoy* women, *all* women, it isn't for their intellect or their warm caring hearts. I want a man who will love only *me!*" Kat pointed to the list. "About number seven . . . I have to admit you have a dry kind of macabre wit. But I'm looking for light-hearted banter, ride the roller-coaster kind of humor."

"You can't fault me on number eight. I have no problem with your job."

"True, but there's also number nine—"

"Okay, okay!" Rourke glared at the list. She'd sliced and diced his personality and found him wanting. He raised his eyes and met her rock solid gaze. "I'm Mr. Wrong."

"Rourke, I want a husband. A man who will love me, love Tory, and meets most if not all my criteria. That's who'll be Mr. Right."

Rourke shuddered. Who in their right mind wanted to marry? Kat of all people should know better. Forget the fact she worked with him daily on his divorce cases, her own marriage had been seven years of hell. In fact, he suspected she'd felt too much relief at Mark's death to mourn. So why this sudden desire to get married?

He glanced at her and silently swore. Tory! Kat would never have an affair or live with a man. She'd be too worried about the effect on her daughter. "I'll help you." His mouth dropped open. Had he said that? And he called himself a lawyer.

"That's okay. You don't need to." Kat pushed back from the table, walked to the kitchen sink, and began rinsing their plates. "I shouldn't have brought it up."

He should have expected this ambush. Even as a kid she'd been unrelenting about getting what she wanted. Right now, she wanted his help. If he didn't give it, she'd find someone else who would. Rourke gritted his teeth. He knew men. They were all dogs on the prowl. Men wanted only one thing and he should know. He was the pack leader.

"We'll start immediately."

Kat turned and glared at him. "I don't want your pity, Rourke."

Rourke grimaced. "Good. You don't have it. I'm a friend. Friends help friends."

"Look. Make sure you're sincere. I need all the help I can get, because so far I haven't mastered the right technique."

"Technique?" Rourke's mouth suddenly felt as dry as a legal brief.

"For attracting men. I don't want another Mark. I've had that." Kat walked over to the table and patted his shoulder. "I understand your hesitation. It'll be hard transforming from boss and friend to instructor in the art of catching a husband."

Rourke's gaze met Kat's, and his world tipped on its axis.

The woman pitied him. Him! The master of seduction. She'd never come close to what she wanted unless she had lessons from "The King." "I'll help. But remember that when we go out it's a real date. And it might change our friendship."

"Oh, come on, Rourke, be honest. You aren't reluctant to help because you're worried about our friendship. It's our work relationship you're scared about. Look, it'll help if you don't view our outings as dates. Think of them as training missions."

He straightened and looked out the kitchen window. "There'll be limits to what I'm willing to do. And I'll set those limits. Agreed?"

"Agreed. Thank you."

"Don't thank me 'til we give it a try. We'll start tomorrow night with a movie."

"Great!"

"I'll call in the morning and set the time." Turning, Rourke walked to the car. It would be a piece of cake. What could go wrong at the movies?

Rourke eased into the aisle seat next to Kat's. "Sorry it took so long," he said, balancing two colas and a giant tub of buttered popcorn. "Here's yours." He handed Kat the diet cola. "The line gets longer and the customers younger every time I go to the movies."

"A sure sign of advancing senility." Kat reached over and slid her fingers into the warm, buttery popcorn. "Of course, you're almost two decades older than most of the audience," she continued as she dropped a few kernels in her mouth.

"Kat—"

"Shush, the movie's about to start."

"Yeah, well at thirty-one, you aren't a spring chicken yourself," Rourke muttered. He grabbed a handful of popcorn and jammed it in his mouth. It wasn't as if thirty-eight was over the hill. "I'm just entering my prime," he mumbled into his straw before taking a swallow of his drink.

"Ah, yes, Prime USDA beef, aged."

Rourke leaned over. "Lesson number one: Don't insult your date, especially about age and appearance. We men tend to be touchy about those subjects. And we sure as hell don't appreciate our dates laughing at us."

Kat patted his hand. "Sorry I hurt your itty-bitty ego."

"Lesson number two: Don't patronize your date for all of the above reasons." Rourke moved the tub to the middle of his lap and stared straight at the screen where the latest heart-throb moaned over some woman.

Romance! "This movie's crap, Kat."

"Stop whining. Just because romance isn't something you believe in doesn't make this a bad movie."

Rourke scowled. So he liked action films and hated melo-dramatic love story drivel. One thing his work as a divorce lawyer had taught him was not to believe in happily ever-afters. They were the exception, not the rule.

He stretched and flung an arm around the back of Kat's chair, hitting the man next to her. Embarrassed, he molded his hand around Kat's upper arm.

"Sit still. You're driving me crazy," Kat hissed at him.

"Sorry." With a grimace, he settled back to watch the screen. As the male star made his move on the blonde bomb-shell, Rourke's interest perked up. Ah, this is more like it, he thought as the torrid love scene unfolded. It was about time they got to the good stuff.

Damn, this actor was good! Rourke felt the woman's hot breath on his face. He imagined himself kneading her volup-tuous body, relishing the feel and weight of her full breasts.

Kat delivered a wicked elbow to his ribs. "Stop that!"

Rourke froze, unable to breathe. What the . . . With a jolt, he realized his fingers were massaging the side of Kat's breast. Mesmerized, he focused on the sensation of her filling his hand. Without thinking, he gave one more squeeze.

"Rourke, stop it!"

Jerking his hand away, he stared straight ahead. It took all his willpower not to adjust his pants.

Damn, he *was* too old for this!

Two hours later, Rourke congratulated himself on his self-control. It'd been a fluke. He'd never have copped a feel if not for that scene in the movie. Kat didn't interest him. At least, not in that way. Never had and never would.

Then he glanced up from his brownie topped with a hot-fudge sundae as Kat's tongue licked the melting sides of her cone in a slow, sensuous movement. *What else can that tongue do?*

Rourke gave himself a mental shake. Nothing like sitting in Baskin-Robbins and thinking about a double-dip in the sheets.

"What's wrong?" Kat asked, dabbing chocolate ice cream from her lips with a napkin. "You aren't still embarrassed are you?"

"About what?" At her raised eyebrow, he forged ahead. "I was thinking about your snide comment. Thirty-eight isn't old."

"Not for tortoises."

Rourke didn't like her deadpan delivery, or her laughing green eyes.

"Come on, Rourke, you *have* slowed down. You used to go out on the town all the time with a beautiful woman on each arm. It's been a while since Liz or I've seen you on a date."

"That's because I'm particular about the company I keep." Kat's assessment of his doddering image infuriated him. Worse, the fact he couldn't set aside the memory of her breast in his hand, more than annoyed him. It frustrated the hell out of him.

It was Kat's fault. If she hadn't written that list and asked for his help, he'd still be seeing her as his kid sister's best friend.

"Come on, Rourke. You're particular about the company you keep, and what?"

"You're not going to let this go, are you?" At Kat's smile, Rourke answered in a tone heavy with wry, self-deprecation, "I only go for refined, well-dressed women of culture and breeding. Of course, a great body and long legs doesn't hurt either." He scooped up a bite of double brownie fudge, and popped it in his mouth.

"A great body, huh?"

Rourke threw his napkin down and started to stand. He didn't need to hear another wise-ass remark.

Kat grabbed his hand. "I've got to know something. Mark always said I was as flat as a pre-teen boy." Kat plopped her cone down in Rourke's plastic bowl. Releasing his hand, she stuck out her chest. "Am I flat or are my boobs large enough to attract men?"

Rourke choked. What did she think? Hadn't he just copped a squeeze in the movies? "Where's your damned common sense?"

"Forget common sense," Kat said. "You're supposed to be my teacher and help me learn the ropes. Now, do you agree with Mark?" She narrowed her eyes and glared at him. "Are they too small?"

"You aren't planning on doing something stupid like getting implants, are you?"

"Of course not!" Once again she straightened her shoulders and thrust out her chest. "So, am I large enough or do I need a Wonderbra?"

The last thing he needed was to stare at Kat's chest, especially with the feel of her breast branded in his mind. Rourke attempted to sidestep with true lawyer skill. "It's hard to tell what your figure's like."

"What do you mean?"

"Kat," Rourke said with a shake of his head, "everything you wear is three sizes too big. You look like a frump."

"A frump? You see me as a frump?"

He blinked at her careful tone. He hadn't meant to destroy her spirit, only change the subject. *And zing her a little,* a small voice whispered inside him. "You're a beautiful woman," Rourke said. "But you hide it."

"You're right." Kat smoothed a hand over her hair. "My hair style isn't much better, is it?"

He sighed in resignation. "Doesn't that bun give you migraines?"

"It's professional." Her mouth firmed, determination written in her cool gaze. "But I'll work on it. Starting tomorrow."

CHAPTER TWO

Kat fingered the sleeve of her blouse. "Come on, Liz, it isn't that bad."

"It's worse." Liz grimaced at the hanging clothes. "It's a disaster."

Kat studied the contents of her closet. "It's all my fault."

"Give yourself a break, Kat. Most of it's Mark's fault. He demanded you wear shapeless clothing. So to keep the peace, you did."

"Yeah, but he's dead and I'm still dressing to suit him. Even my jeans are baggy. Not the teenage style of over-sized, studied sloppy, but pre-grunge." Kat jerked the excess fabric of her pants leg out four inches. "I never knew how bad I looked until the other night. Rourke's words hurt, but they were right on the money."

Liz shook her head. "Leave it to my brother to use his usual tact and diplomacy."

"I need blunt honesty, not tact." She shrugged, backed up and collapsed onto her bed. "A good swift kick in the butt. Starting now, old habits are pitched and new ones are on the agenda." Kat hesitated, then jumped back up and marched over to her closet. She waved at its contents. "Is there anything here you think is salvageable?"

Liz pitched everything onto the floor. Moments later, she surveyed the littered carpet and picked up a narrow black-leather belt between her thumb and forefinger. "You can keep this. Good belts are hard to find."

Kat's gaze flew between the empty closet and the floor.

Suddenly cold and clammy, she fell backwards on the bed, dollar signs circling before her eyes.

Liz dumped the contents of her Burger Hut bag in the trash can and slapped the open paper sack over Kat's mouth. "Breathe deeply, you're hyperventilating."

Kat took several deep breaths, then eased into a sitting position. "Rourke claims you have 'Born to Shop' tattooed on your forehead. Prove it, oh wise one. My body is in your hands." She glanced down at the floor and felt the creeping clamminess begin again. "Just keep it below my bankruptcy threshold, okay?"

"Will do." Liz tipped Kat's face up toward hers. "The minute you don't take my advice, the deal is off."

A tremor shot through Kat. She knew years from now she still wouldn't be able to say if it was caused by fear or expectation. "I'll be a good girl." Kat saluted Liz. "Girl Scouts' promise."

Liz stepped back and studied Kat, then motioned her to stand. She walked around Kat, examining her. "You also said Rourke made a couple of snide comments about your hair."

"My hair's fine. I can't have long hair hanging in my face all day. I'm not the straight flip-over-your shoulder kinda gal as is Clarissa, the owl."

"Agreed," Liz laughed. "But that doesn't mean you don't need a new 'do.' " She frowned. "Come to think of it, the rest of you could use an overhaul, too."

"You make it sound like I'm going in for a three-thousand mile oil change with lube and grease job."

"Not too far from it." Liz pointed a finger. "You, my good friend, are about to show your assets, not keep them hidden like your clients. Even Rourke knew better than to insult your body. You've got a great one. Your problem is you don't flaunt what nature gave you. But I know how to fix it. We don't start with a clothes-shopping spree. We start with the basics of a body makeover."

"My body?" Kat looked down. "That'll take more than one day."

"Not with Henri's help."

"You jest, Elizabeth. Henri is good, but *ma cherié* there are limits to even my outstanding talents." Henri stood a foot away from the chair where Kat sat, hand on his hip, face scrunched in a frown of concentration.

"You have the ability to see the swan beneath the surface, Henri, and let the world discover what's been hidden. I know what you did for Barbara before her wedding. Then there was Monica before the hearing . . ."

"Ah, but, *cherié*, enough money always accentuates my God-given abilities."

"You, my dear, are a tease. Too bad you don't like women."

He slapped a hand over his chest. "I adore them, Elizabeth. Absolutely *love* them." He walked across the floor, his hips in a seductive sway, and paused close to Kat's chair. "With enough time—" He paused, took a deep breath. "And enough patience, even *this* I can transform."

"Gee, don't kill yourself going overboard with the compliments." Kat propped her face up with her elbow. "This is a waste of time, Liz. I'm a lost cause."

"Henri, I have a proposal for you." Liz gestured to Kat. "Let me have that hundred dollar bill."

"What hundred dollar bill?"

"The one tucked under the flap in your wallet." Liz turned to Henri. "She's such an accountant. Parts slowly with her cash. You should see her. Her life may be in total disarray, but she keeps her money neatly stacked in the same direction and carefully placed in denominational order."

"Ah, *ma cherié*, with you beside her that will no doubt change."

"You better believe it. The bill." Liz held out her hand.

Kat glared at Liz. She couldn't believe it. First Rourke, now Liz had turned on her. "Not a chance."

"Come on, Kat. Don't wuss out on me. Hand it over."

Scowling, Kat opened up her purse, jerked her wallet free, and removed a crisp one hundred-dollar bill. "Here." She held it out. As Liz started to take it, Kat's grip tightened.

"Kaaaat!"

With a sniff, Kat released the bill. "There goes the next ten trips to the movies, including buttered popcorn."

"You'll make your own full-length features. Besides you don't need the butter." Liz waved the bill in front of Henri's nose. "If you do what I know you can, you get this in addition to your regular fee."

"Liz," Kat gasped.

"I'll pay it," Liz shot back. "And it'll be worth it to see you like you should be." She turned toward Henri. "I don't want a gloss-over. I want a new woman. One who oozes sensuality. A woman who with one look could sink a fleet of cabin cruisers. Got my drift?"

"I cannot promise sex, *m'amie,* only the semblance of passion, hot wild nights and the image of a woman ready to be pressed close against her *amour.*"

"That'll do just fine."

Kat pressed her hand over her pounding heart. Could he do it? Could Henri create that new Kat without first performing a lobotomy?

Afraid to move, Kat sat ram-rod straight in her chair as three women worked simultaneously on different parts of her body. One knelt at her feet putting the final touches on a pedicure. Another applied a clear top-coat over the dark-pink nail polish on her fingernails, while the third woman patted translucent powder on her face.

This was the most relaxed Kat had been in the past four hours. After she'd gotten over the shock of seeing stretches of her waist-length hair fall to the floor, the haircut seemed a painless procedure. How was she supposed to know that was just the beginning?

The next three and half hours were spent bouncing between nirvana and hell. The salt-rub, mud-wrap and facial were heaven. The massage, the deep massage that made her muscles scream, was hell. Then just when she'd settled back into the heaven of a peaceful mineral bath, the three Gestapo surrounding her had demanded she towel off so they could assault anew.

"I feel like an assembly-line vehicle," Kat said as the make-up artist patted her chin one last time.

"Don't talk. It'll mess up your finish."

Kat rolled her eyes. "Just don't make it a spit and polish."

"Ah, your transformation is complete, *cherié*." Henri sashayed into the room with two other men. "Please forgive me, but I must show my colleagues the finished product." He tipped her chin first one direction, then another. "I believe you, my dear, are my best work of art ever."

Kat slid a glance over at the two men who had arrived with Henri. The man carrying a camera stood no more than five-feet tall and had long, slicked back hair. The other one had tattooed eyebrows, wore one, long hoop earring, and had long, painted fingernails. "Oh, Henri, you are the master. There is no question," the man with the tattooed eyebrows lisped.

"Let us see what her friend thinks."

Henri walked from the room and the petite cameraman began to snap photos. "Please, miss, let Henri have permission to use these pictures. He will run away with the next Beautician's Expo."

"As what, 'beast is transformed'?"

"Praise God and pass the ammunition."

Kat spun her chair toward Liz standing in the doorway. Mid-turn she paused and stared at the stunning stranger in the mirror.

"I do believe you're almost ready. That is, as soon as you stop imitating a flytrap, and we buy that new wardrobe," Liz said with a chuckle.

Kat handed Rourke's secretary, Grace, a file. "If he has any questions, I'll be in my office."

"I like the change, Kat. You look great."

"Thanks." She patted her French braid in lieu of tugging at the end of her short, straight skirt. It might only be two inches above her knee, but it felt like six.

Why had she blindly followed Liz's advice? She'd have thought alarm bells would have gone off when Liz had deemed one narrow black belt the only item in her wardrobe salvageable. But no. She'd gotten caught up in the "let's overhaul Kat" fever and had ordered Liz to give everything to the women's shelter.

No backsliding for her. No siree. So what had it gained her, besides feeling awkward? Zip. Nada. Not a blasted thing.

So far, Rourke hadn't noticed the change. Kat frowned. She needed him to notice. Because if her tutor didn't see any difference, the men she was hunting sure wouldn't.

Moments later, Rourke barged through the law firm's outer doors. As he approached her, Kat thrust out her chest, retrieved the files from Grace's desk, and handed them to

21

Rourke. "My findings on the Chambers' case."

"Thanks." Rourke glanced at Grace. "Send Bruce in as soon as he arrives. I'll need you, too, Kat." Pivoting, he walked into his office, reading the file.

Kat bit her lower lip. Maybe she should have worn the tight knit tee with the skirt instead of the silk. Still, Liz had insisted the sheer, lavender blouse——which needed a camisole under it to make it decent—was the thing to wear with the black skirt.

A shrill whistle pierced the air as Bruce Chambers entered the room. "Wow!" His eyes drifted down to Kat's chest and stopped. "Good thing you work for a lawyer, beautiful, 'cause the way you look should be against the law."

Kat grinned. She wasn't surprised Bruce had noticed. This made the fourth time in ten years he'd come to Rourke for a divorce. "Rourke's expecting you."

"He's always expecting me."

"You know, Mr. Chambers, all this could have been avoided if you'd followed your attorney's advice and gotten a prenuptial."

"I know. Trouble is, it's impossible to think contracts when you're busy with contraceptive matters. Ya know?" Bruce winked again. "That's why Rourke's on retainer."

He leaned against the desk. "I got the documents Rourke wanted. They prove I owned the *Trophy II* before Milly and I were married." As Bruce handed Kat a folder, the back of his fingers brushed against her blouse. "Too bad you can't wear this outfit every day. Did you buy any more?"

Kat sighed. Bruce thought with only one head, and it sure wasn't the one on top of his shoulders. Witness his marriage to Milly, not to mention Sally and Bunny before her. Bunny. Wouldn't you think he'd have a clue? Kat couldn't stop her slow, wicked grin.

"I just realized something, Mr. Chambers. All your wives names end with a 'y'. Hmm." She tapped her index finger against her lips. "I wonder what Freud or Jung would say."

"That I'm attracted to bimbos?" His gaze slid over her accompanied by another shrill whistle. "But I'm willing to move up the intellectual ladder. Want to help me?"

Kat didn't know which was worse, Bruce Chambers' leer or loud wolf whistle. She glanced uneasily at Rourke's closed door. Suddenly it jerked open.

"Why the cat-calls?" Rourke asked, coming out of his office.

"Ah," Bruce said, moving his eyebrows up and down. "Appropriate name, Kat-calls."

As Rourke's slow assessing gaze perused her body, Kat blushed and perspiration dampened her face. She didn't know whether to scream or laugh. First Bruce and now Rourke stared at her chest. The difference lay in the reaction. Bruce's had been one of appreciation, not a grimace.

"Grace, would you please show Mr. Chambers into my office and wait for me. I'll need you to take notes."

Bruce laughed. "What's the matter? Afraid the better man will whisk her away?" He winked in Kat's direction before turning to follow Grace. "If you have any problems, you can come work for me, beautiful."

At the door's snap, Rourke turned back to Kat. "Nice Wonderbra. And what the hell happened to your skirt?" He picked a pen and memo pad off Grace's desk. "It's only a matter of time before criminal charges are pressed."

"Liz'll love having her big brother defend her." Kat wanted to back up at Rourke's advance. Instead, she stiffened her spine, ignored his glare of censure and met his gaze head-on. "Yup. It took the weekend, but we've picked out an entirely new wardrobe."

She slid her hands down her hips. "I like this new look. Don't you?"

Rourke leaned down, his nose almost touching hers. "What new look?" he asked, his deep voice a growl. "A strip of spandex covered by a flimsy scrap of cloth?"

Kat scowled up at Rourke. "It's better than looking like a frump."

"There's a happy medium between frump and red-light district."

She stared at him. She'd be darned if she'd let him get to her. Liz had warned her Rourke might be difficult. He didn't like change, unless he supervised it. She looked professional. Nordstrom didn't sell anything but professional. At least, not when shopping with a buyer. "Forget B.B. Blue's. Friday's off."

Rourke's gaze stayed on her chest. "We're still on." He turned and stalked back to his office.

CHAPTER THREE

Fuming, Rourke headed back to his table at B.B. Blue's. He'd brought Kat here thinking they'd have a relaxed evening of dancing and conversation. Once he had her laughing, he'd planned to tackle the subject of her outrageous dress the past week. What a joke.

Tonight the B.B. in B.B. Blue's might as well stand for *Bye-bye Baby*.

He couldn't hit the john without returning to find a dog sniffing at his territory, and here was another. This one looked like a puppy. Rourke stopped beside Kat's chair and rested his hand on her shoulder. He glared down at the youngster who'd joined Kat at their table. The kid looked like he should be home doing his homework.

"I'll tell you what I told my last patient, you don't need implants."

Rourke struggled to maintain his courtroom expression. "You're a doctor?"

"Resident, second year."

"Attorney, fourteenth year." Rourke suppressed a grin. The puppy almost wet the floor. With a curt nod, Rourke grabbed Kat's hand and jerked her to her feet. "Let's dance."

Not waiting for her answer, he towed her onto the small, intimate dance floor. Drawing her close, he swayed in time to the slow, lazy beat of the blues and tried to regain his composure.

"You weren't nice to Tom, back there."

Rourke missed a step and came down on Kat's foot. "Sorry."

"You should be. Attorney, fourteenth year. Jeez, Rourke, what's gotten into you."

"Nothing, not a damned thing." He pulled her flush against him. Monday, it had been the skirt and sheer blouse. Hell, every day she'd shown up in a new outfit. Each outfit served as another showcase for her lush figure and legs that went to her armpits.

Then there was the makeup. Not too much—just enough to make her eyes stand out bright green against long, thick black lashes.

Rourke's hand caressed Kat's bare back. Damned dress. She deserved her time in the sun, but in this dress she'd get burned. It screamed "I'm yours," to every guy still breathing. Forget that, it'd get a rise out of a corpse.

"Your dress is drawing every man's attention, including the blind one in the corner," he said as his fingers slipped down her exposed back. It'd be so easy to slip lower, beneath the edge of her dress and cup her nice, tight bottom.

Kat pulled back just in time. "There's nothing wrong with my dress!"

He arched an eyebrow at her carefully bit-off words and smiled. "Really? Doogie Houser was ready to trade his stethoscope for one feel."

Rourke winced as her precisely placed heel came down on his instep. "Before you accept any dates, talk to me," he growled.

"I'm thirty-one and old enough to say *yes* without permission."

"You asked for my help, and that's what you're getting."

"No. That's not what I'm getting. I'm getting harassed."

Rourke wanted to shake her. Didn't she understand the

effect she had on men? He looked down into pools of wide, green innocence and groaned. "You're a rookie when it comes to single men. Mark nabbed you before you'd finished your first season. In the last decade, the game's changed. That's why I stay in the dugout. It isn't safe out in the field."

"Afraid I'll hit a foul ball, or is it the grand slam you're worried about?"

"Neither." Rourke pulled Kat back tight against his chest. "Just listen to your coach."

"Rourke?"

"Yes?"

"I don't feel like fighting. Tonight's been one of the best of my life."

Rourke missed another step. "Sure, no problem. Look, you're almost ready for the majors." At Kat's perplexed gaze, Rourke said, "Bruce Chambers wants you."

"Oh, him," Kat shrugged. "He's nice enough. Even if he met my criteria, which he doesn't, I wouldn't be interested. His track record is worse than yours." She shuddered. "He not only beds his mistakes, he marries them—even one named Bunny."

What was going on? Kat was his friend and employee, nothing more. So why was he muttering a prayer of thanks?

As soon as the combo finished their number, Rourke wrenched his fingers from her bare back and glanced at his watch. "It's almost midnight. Time we headed home." He guided Kat off the dance floor with his hand resting just above the curve of her tight, round bottom.

"Can't we stay longer? I don't have a curfew. Tory's spending the night at Liz's, remember?"

Rourke slid a glance at her bottom. "I'm beat." He wanted out of there. He caught another leer and glared the man down. "As you pointed out at the movies, I'm over the hill." At Kat's mock scowl and playful punch in the arm, Rourke chuckled. "Seriously, it's been a hellacious week and we've got a big day tomorrow."

"How could I have forgotten tomorrow's excursion?"

"Too involved fielding admirers," he mumbled under his breath.

Thirty minutes later, they stood on Kat's porch. Rourke took her key and opened the front door.

"Rourke." Kat reached out and grabbed his arm. "Thank you for the lovely evening, over-protective big brother routine and all."

"Don't mention it." Rourke looked down into Kat's gleaming eyes and felt his stomach drop. Right now, at this moment, the last thing he wanted from this sexy woman was friendship. "Get some sleep. Our trip tomorrow begins early." Rourke groaned at the passion her gaze promised.

One kiss and he'd be cured. His lips slowly descended and covered her lips in a feather-soft caress. He'd been right. He felt nothing. He started to lift his mouth.

Her arms wrapped around his neck and deepened the kiss. He heard her low moan as she pressed herself closer to him. Suddenly, he realized it was his, not her, groan.

Shocked, Rourke eased himself away and moved back two steps. He shoved his hands in his trousers' front pockets. "About tomorrow, I'll swing by Liz's for Tory and pick you up at ten."

"Thanks for being such a good teacher." She slid inside and closed the door behind her.

"Who's teaching whom?" Rourke muttered as he turned and walked back to his car.

Kat glared at the kitchen clock in disgust. It was almost eight and she'd been awake since six. What sleep she'd gotten had been fitful and disjointed, broken by dreams of a highly erotic nature—dreams in Panavision, brilliant color and Sur-round-sound.

She couldn't shake the memory of one of them. She could still feel Rourke's feather-like touch on her skin, his tongue caressing her lips before it went on to explore her ear and neck—kissing, nibbling . . .

"Oh, Lordy," Kat muttered. What was she thinking? He was her best friend's older brother. Heck, all her life she'd thought of him as the older brother she'd never had! That's how he saw himself. So why did she feel on edge and filled with anticipation when around him?

Last night his low voice had dissolved her will with the same ease a stack of hot pancakes melted whipped butter. Damn and blast the man. It was his fault she felt shivers down her spine and tingling in the pit of her stomach.

Kat shook her head. It didn't take an accountant looking at the balance sheet to know she was in trouble. The moment she'd kissed him, she had entered an emotional minefield from which there was no safe exit. Something told her that these feelings, once awakened, weren't easily buried. Still, she could try to bury those dreams so deep they'd surface in China.

The ringing telephone startled her. Kat glanced at the kitchen clock. Eight-thirty. No one called this early on a Saturday morning.

Unless it was Rourke . . . calling to cancel. That was a pos-sibility. A hoped for possibility. Kat set her diet cola down, rose from her chair and grabbed the phone. "Yes?"

"Hey."

Kat's stomach churned. She took a deep breath and slowly released it. "I figured it was either you or Tory. What's up?"

"I called to let you know I'm at Liz's. We've finished eating breakfast. Tory and I should be there within thirty minutes."

Kat grabbed the ladder-back chair and struggled to regain her equilibrium. "It's only eight-thirty."

"I have a watch."

"I can't be ready in thirty minutes."

"Don't worry, Tory, your mom'll be ready when we get there."

"Forget it, Rourke. I won't be ready for at least an hour."

"We aren't going to a symphony. Just throw on a pair of jeans. We'll be there in thirty minutes."

At the buzzing in her ear, Kat slammed the receiver onto the hook and tore up the stairs to her bedroom. Moments later, she stood thunderstruck, staring at the image in the bathroom mirror.

"It's a joke, right?" she muttered, reaching out and touching her reflection. "Oh, God, I look like a character out of *The Night of the Living Dead*."

She needed something to shock her system into wakefulness and she knew just the thing to do it. She reached into the shower and turned the blue knob on high.

Freezing to death was better than looking like a zombie. Grimacing, she eased under the icy spray. With her luck, she'd end up looking like a ghoul with a bad case of goose pimples.

"Suffering's an over-rated commodity. Time for sauna conditions." Kat twisted the hot water tap on high and the cold down to dribble.

Once out of the shower, she quickly toweled off and checked herself for some improvement. Oh, joy! Upgraded from zombie to intensive care patient.

Praise the Lord that under Liz's patient tutelage she'd conquered the use of cosmetics. Kat grabbed her make-up kit. Desperate times called for desperate measures, she thought, applying an extra coat of concealer to the purple shadows beneath her eyes. Finished, she stood back from the mirror and surveyed the results. "Could be worse. Been worse," Kat muttered with a scowl as she secured her long, damp hair in a French braid.

Her robe flapping at her heels, Kat fled the steamy bathroom and rushed to her closet. Without looking, she jerked the first outfit her hands touched from the rack.

She'd just shimmied into a pair of pale yellow linen walking-shorts when the front door slammed and small running feet pounded up the stairs. Kat sighed as Tory burst through her bedroom door.

"Uncle Rourke's in the car, Mommy. An' he said you've had plenty of time to get ready, so move your butt."

"Stow it, Tory."

"Are you all right, Mommy? You don't look so good."

"I'm fine," she snapped. "Do me a favor, stop talking about how bad I look."

"Okie dokie. But I bet Uncle Rourke's gonna say somethin'. He *always* notices when you don't feel good."

And always points it out! Kat retrieved her purse and sunglasses from the bathroom counter. Then, firmly grasping Tory's shoulder, Kat escorted her down to Rourke and his waiting car.

Please Lord, let everything be back to normal.

One quick glance told Rourke Kat's night had been as restless as his. This business of coaching her how to attract a man had kept *him* up all night. Not even a dozen cold showers could have quieted his raging imagination. He still couldn't believe he'd told her that before long she'd be ready to date.

He didn't want to see Kat hurt. He wanted her happy. She deserved it. He wanted to keep her safe, yet help her find Mr. Right. But how could he accomplish both when they were mutually exclusive? Damn, he hated Catch 22 situations.

Rourke drummed his fingers on the steering wheel. After last night, he knew how easy it would be to cross the line from friend to lover. He grabbed the steering wheel and squeezed. If he ever felt her soft, yielding lips again, he wouldn't stop. As with potato chips, one of Kat's kisses wasn't enough.

Forcing down his frustration, Rourke glanced at Kat's still profile. "Are you feeling up to the trip to Harpers Ferry?"

"Of course," she said, staring straight ahead.

"Are you sure? We can postpone until tomorrow."

She took a slow, deep breath and then let it out. "You're the one who wanted an early start. Put it in gear, and let's get going."

Rourke backed out of the driveway. "What's the matter? Exhausted?"

"Just drive." She sank back against her seat.

"Well?"

"I didn't sleep well."

Rourke grinned. Good! Why should he be the only one to suffer? "You've always said nothing disturbs your sleep."

"I was planning my future, and since I'm now officially in training, the anticipation of learning kept me awake."

"Oh? And what are you learning, Kat?"

Kat pulled her glasses down her nose and looked over the top of the frames. "You tell me. What's your lesson plan for the day?"

"No lesson plan for today, just games." His lips twitched. "But can I trust you to follow the rules?"

"Suck eggs," she hissed.

Tory bounced up and down in her seat. "How much longer?"

Rourke pinched the bridge of his nose. "For the third time

in as many minutes, as soon as I find a parking space." He ground his teeth. *Where's a roll of Duck Tape when you need it?* "Plant yourself and stay buckled until we stop!"

"There's a spot!" Tory yelled, pointing, almost clipping his nose.

It was a coveted spot by the river. "Good going, Tory. It's perfect," Rourke said with forced good cheer as he flipped on his signal light.

"Did you see that? I had my blinker on and that son-of-a-bitch stole my space! Hell, I'd even started my turn!"

Kat raised her window. "Rourke! Watch your language. Tory's in the car."

"Yup, he stole your space, all right," Tory agreed in a solemn tone.

Rourke lowered his window further.

Tory followed suit and lowered hers. Kat turned and lunged for her daughter, just missing her. "Victoria Danielle Snow, if you open your mouth, even to breathe, you're grounded from TV for the next year. Sit down *now* and raise that window!"

Rourke frowned. Just what he needed, his sole supporter grounded. What would Kat threaten him with, loss of dating privileges?

"Forget this space, Rourke. I've got parking karma. Start cruising the lot."

"Parking karma?" Rourke asked with a snicker.

"Mommy really does. We always get spaces right in front of the mall. Even the day before Christmas."

"Men." Kat wrinkled her nose at his raised brow. "You're all hunters. It's in your genes. Everything's a competition, even parking."

"What? So now my whole sex is being maligned?"

Kat shrugged. "The truth hurts. There." She pointed to a

place fifteen feet closer to the river. "I told you. I have parking karma."

A few minutes later, Rourke helped Kat out of the car and swallowed a groan. No doubt about it, he should have followed his instincts last night and canceled today. Hell, he should have voided the entire deal. The contract was untenable. They were co-workers. She was his sister's best friend. How could he have agreed to this? Because she asked, a small voice answered.

Extricating himself from this mess would prove costly. If he didn't handle it just right, he stood to lose everything, including his sister's and Kat's respect.

Rourke slanted a glance in Kat's direction. Restraint wasn't in the cards. Ever since embarking on this fool's errand, all he could think of was seducing her. He swore to himself that before the day was out he'd regain his control.

Kat took several deep breaths to relieve her tension. It didn't work. The man was suddenly impossible to read. She found herself questioning every word Rourke said, reviewing every sound he made.

She never should have asked for his help. Darn Liz. She'd played on Kat's longing to find a husband, a Mr. Right, who would also be a loving stepfather for Tory. Liz and her double blasted ideas. Kat had known it was a bad idea from the start. Of course, it hadn't helped, that Liz was a shrink and knew how to punch all her buttons.

Rubbing her thumb across her fingers, she could still feel the heat of his skin from where she'd touched him. She shook her head. *Transference. Yeah, that's what it was, transference.* She was misplacing her affections, putting them off on her teacher.

Rourke slammed the BMW's trunk closed. "Liz packed a

lunch for us." He handed Kat the basket.

Raising the lid, she peered inside. "By the looks of it, she had help from the deli," Kat said, her lips twitching as her gaze met his.

"I helped! We got really good stuff, Mommy."

At Tory's serious expression, Kat smothered a laugh. "You certainly did."

"Lead the way, Tory. We'll follow. Be sure to pick a shady spot near the water," Rourke called.

As they walked together toward the riverbank, Kat's hand brushed Rourke's. She flashed him a smile. His pewter-gray gaze burned into hers. A tremor ran through her body along with the memory of her fitful night. *Down girl. Don't forget why you asked for his help. Remember your goal.*

Fifteen minutes later, Kat reclined on the blanket, her legs stretched out before her. Smiling, she watched Tory and Rourke play with a Frisbee.

In spite of the cracks she'd made to the contrary, the years had been kind to him. The hint of gray at his temples made him more handsome than during his youth. Rourke, she decided, was one of that rare breed of men who looked fantastic in a suit or a well-worn pair of 501's. As he bent to retrieve the Frisbee, she wondered what it would feel like to stroke his nice, tight buns. To run her hands down his muscular thighs.

Transference. Remember, it's just transference, Kat reminded herself. She forced herself to focus on his and Tory's bantering over the best way to skip rocks on the river.

Kat watched them play. Rourke liked Tory, and she loved him.

Blast and double blast!

Rourke passed the Tory test!

CHAPTER FOUR

Rourke watched Kat's eyes soften as Tory ran back to the river's edge and her newfound friends. It reminded him of when, after Mark's death, Kat had returned home and he'd asked her if she'd ever regretted marrying Mark. Her answer had been a quick and emphatic, "No. I have Tory."

He agreed with Kat about Tory and would kill to protect the little girl. He also felt a deep sadness at the humiliation Kat had suffered during her marriage. He knew all about the effects of a partner's repeated infidelity. He saw the results in his office daily.

Kat had deserved better than that sleaze. To this day, Rourke didn't understand why she'd stayed with the rat.

Yes, he did. Pride. Kat was a walking advertisement of the price excess pride extracts. The woman had shown an overabundance of that commodity since childhood and still allowed it to rule her. When Kat's back was against the wall, her stubbornness kicked in and decisions were based strictly on salvaging her pride. Witness how his true but caustic remarks had driven her straight into Mark's arms.

When would she learn pride wasn't everything? He snorted. Probably never. Too bad he couldn't teach her how he kept from letting it rule his life. Rourke popped the rest of his sandwich into his mouth.

He'd learned his lesson. He'd teach the fledgling to fly, then bow out gracefully and keep his opinions about the men she dated to himself.

Kat's laugher interrupted his thoughts.

"It's great seeing her like this. She's running, jumping, and laughing. All because of you." Kat flashed Rourke a look filled with gratitude and relief.

Rourke felt his ears begin to burn. "Here," he mumbled, offering her one of the peaches they'd bought at a roadside stand.

"Thanks." Kat took the fruit from his outstretched hand. "Mm, this is good. I haven't eaten one this ripe or sweet in a long time."

Rourke watched Kat bite into the succulent fruit. He swallowed hard at the sight of peach juice coating her lips. His tongue mimicked Kat's as she tried to catch the liquid, dripping from the corner of her mouth. He hesitated briefly, then with a groan that sounded like a muffled curse, he slid his hand around the nape of her fragile neck and held her still.

Using his thumb, he lifted her chin and stared into her wide green eyes. "So sweet," he murmured. As he bent his head, her breath brushed his lips. His mind screamed, "Whoa, boy! Stop! Off limits!" Taking a deep breath, Rourke pulled back and muttered an apology.

"Oh, my God!" Kat jumped to her feet. "Tory! Don't move!"

Rourke turned and spotted Tory standing on a high stone wall. As he vaulted to his feet, he saw Tory's foot slip. He prayed her grasp on the ledge held. The thought of her falling and landing on the pebbled beach below sent a shudder through him. In seconds, Rourke passed Kat.

Seconds later, he squatted beside an unmoving Tory, trying to recall his first-aid. It'd been a long time since he'd been an Eagle Scout. Twenty-two years to be exact. But he remembered enough to know you didn't move an injured person.

Kat reached out to draw Tory to her.

"Stay where you are, Katherine! Neither one of us is going

to move her until the paramedics arrive and we know the extent of her injuries." Rourke placed two fingers on the pulse point at Tory's throat. He raised his gaze to Kat's anguish-filled face. "She's got a strong and even pulse."

"Mommy?" Tory lifted her head.

"Oh, Punkin, I was so scared." Kat knelt down beside Tory. "I want you to lay still. Rourke's going to call help."

"I'm okay, Mommy. Really."

"I'm sure you are." Kat's eyes met Rourke's. "But you had a bad fall."

Ignoring Kat's order, Tory started to push herself upright and screamed.

Her wail felt like a knife in Rourke's gut. He placed a restraining hand on her. "Don't move, Tory." Bending over her, he examined her cradled left arm. "It's broken." He glanced at Kat. "Stay here. I'll use the cell phone in the car to call the paramedics."

Rourke rose slowly from his chair, walked outside the emergency room, and stood beside the ambulance's double doors. What was it about hospital antiseptic smells that got to him? It never failed, he always felt claustrophobic, like the walls were closing in on him and the men in white jackets were on their way.

No doubt, Liz would have an explanation for his unwarranted fears—something deep-rooted in his pre-conscious. As far as he was concerned, it only meant he didn't like white walls and antiseptic smells.

As he moved further out into the cool air and the low light of lingering sun rays, Rourke gagged on a cloud of smoke. A half dozen cigarette smokers stood puffing in the last place they were allowed, outdoors.

Rourke shook his head. He tried to focus on mundane

matters, but couldn't. The fact remained, he was responsible for Tory's condition. If only he hadn't been preoccupied with Kat. If only he hadn't wanted her so badly, so shamelessly. If only he'd seen Tory's predicament sooner. If only . . .

Kat hadn't spoken to him since they'd left the beach at Harpers Ferry. For the most part, she sat quietly in the waiting area. Occasionally, she'd jump up and pace, and once in awhile she'd mumble the words, "I can't believe they won't let me back there." But the words weren't directed toward him.

Rourke wiped his damp palms on his jean-clad thighs. Then, squaring his shoulders, he walked back inside the automatic doors to the emergency waiting area and over to Kat.

As he lightly rested his hands on her shoulders, he felt Kat stiffen, then relax. He massaged the tight shoulders and didn't say a word, just inhaled the clean white-apple scent of her hair, thankful it masked the odor of the hospital.

Kat reached up and grabbed one of his hands. She turned with his hand still in hers. Lord, he hated that look of fear on her face.

"I was so afraid, Rourke. I was afraid Tory had died. She was lying there so still. What if I'd lost her?"

Rourke swallowed. "She's just like a small kitten—made of nothing but cartilage. She could probably fall thirty feet and land on her feet unharmed."

Kat's eyes suddenly flared as she dropped Rourke's hand. "I should have known you'd come up with some flippant remark. We're not talking about a pet, here. We're talking about my daughter. But why would I expect anything else from a man who'd rather eat children."

"Only after they're cooked."

"You're insufferable! How could you make a joke at a time like this?"

"Well, I thought it was better than wallowing in self-pity."

"Self-pity! I'm not worried about myself!" Kat glanced over at the woman on the other side of the aisle, then back at Rourke as she lowered her voice. "You bastard."

"I know who my mother was, thank you very much." Rourke stuck his hand in his pants pocket and jingled his change nervously. This conversation was not going the way he'd wanted it to.

Tears filled her eyes. "If you hadn't distracted me from watching out for Tory, she wouldn't have fallen."

Rourke's hands dropped to his sides. His fingers curled into fists. "Nice to know I'm not the only one blaming me."

She shook her head. "I don't really blame you. It was an accident. Although, you didn't help the situation."

"You're the one who sat there with peach juice running down your chin. The one who deliberately enticed me by licking your lips."

"You're the one who gave me the peach. Besides, if your jeans hadn't been so tight across your—I wouldn't have—" Kat held up her hand. "I don't want to do this. I just want my daughter safe."

"You're right." Rourke winced. He hated to apologize for anything to a woman. Especially this one. What made it worse was he really had been the one who'd caused the whole thing.

Rourke saw her eyes fill with tears. Not that she would shed them. Oh, no, Kat was too tough for that. She'd just blink them away. "I'm sorry, Kat."

"No need." She placed a hand on his cheek. "I was out of line. I'm just so scared. What happened wasn't your fault, or mine. Children have accidents all the time. And as a parent, you consider yourself lucky if all they do is break a few bones."

Kat's soft smile faded as she watched his expression tighten. "Rourke, there's no way anyone can watch a child twenty-four hours a day, especially one as active and curious as Tory."

Rourke shifted his weight from foot to foot. "It never should have happened, Kat."

"You're right, it shouldn't have. Tory was showing off. Doing something she knew I wouldn't approve of." Kat sighed. "*We* were both there. And *we* did not abandon Tory."

"You really don't blame me?"

Kat brushed a lock of hair off Rourke's forehead. "Of course, I don't blame you. It was an accident. Nothing more. This isn't Tory's first trip to Harpers Ferry. She knows the drill. As I said, she went somewhere she'd been told not to go and was doing something she'd been expressly forbidden to do."

Rourke felt a heavy weight lifted from his shoulders. He needed to make a joke, lighten the situation. Things were too tense and the desire to touch and hold her was getting out of control. "So, if Tory's accident is the result of her willful disobedience, what's her punishment?"

Kat smiled. "Hugs and kisses."

"That's what I thought. You're a marshmallow. It's going to take someone of stronger stuff than you to devise an appropriate punishment."

"Right." Kat slid her arms around him and laid her head against his chest.

For a minute, Rourke's arms hung loose beside him, then, slowly, he wrapped them around her and held her close. With his thumb, he lifted her chin and brushed her lips with a feather-light kiss, then pulled back from her.

From the abruptness of Kat's withdrawal, he decided the kiss had surprised her just as it had him. But then, he'd never read women well, except in bed. Not that he would ever take Kat there.

"How much longer before someone comes and tells us something? If we were at Fairfax Hospital, they would have let us stay with her."

"I don't know, sweetheart." Rourke nodded in agreement. "But it's only been twenty minutes since Doctor Wade came out and told us they'd have to set her arm."

His words seemed to reassure her. "Still—"

"Be fair to this hospital. I doubt even Fairfax would allow a parent to observe the setting of their child's bone. Most parents don't handle their kids' pain well. Besides, they're probably afraid you'd sue them if Tory felt pain."

No sooner had Rourke finished than the door to Treatment Room Four burst open. Grinning, Doctor Wade covered the distance between them in three long strides. "It's always reassuring to see parents loving and comforting one another and not just their children." Rourke dropped his arms from Kat. *Parent? Not likely!*

"Tory's doing well. She's a trooper. As I told you earlier, she's broken the radius of her left arm but is going to be just fine." Doctor Wade gestured for Kat and Rourke to seat themselves.

"We've just finished casting Tory, so you can visit her in a few minutes. Just be aware that it'll take about thirty minutes for the cast to fully harden. By the way, she's very proud of her cast. It's hot pink," he added, grinning broadly.

"Tory was unconscious for two or three minutes." Rourke gently squeezed Kat's hand. "Does she have a concussion?"

"I didn't see any signs of one." Doctor Wade held up his hand. "She also hasn't experienced any nausea, headaches, or sleepiness while I've been treating her. But just in case, keep an eye on her for the next twenty-four hours. As for her arm, at her age she'll only have the cast on for four weeks."

Doctor Wade reached into his white coat pocket and withdrew a prescription pad. "She needs to be seen by a pediatric orthopedist. When you get home, call Tory's pediatrician for a referral and make an appointment."

He tore a piece of paper from the pad and handed it to Rourke. "Here's a prescription for some pain medication for your daughter. She may need it later today." He paused, then grinned and motioned them to follow him. "I know a little girl who is dying to see you."

Entering Tory's room, Kat's hand sought Rourke's and held it tightly as Tory turned her face toward the door. Looking pale and frightened, she gave her mother and Rourke a small smile. "Can I go home?"

Kat rushed over to Tory. She gently gathered her little girl to her as tears rolled silently down her checks. "Of course you can." Then, sniffling, she kissed Tory's forehead and cheeks while murmuring reassuring endearments.

Hugging them both to him, Rourke swallowed hard and cleared his throat. "We'll leave in a few minutes, sweetheart. Why don't you and I go get the car? Mommy can sign all the papers and get your prescription filled."

"You're not mad at me?" Tory looked hopefully from one to the other.

"No. Just relieved you're going to be as good as new," Kat confessed.

"That's your Mother for you. But me, I'm different. I've already settled on the perfect punishment for scaring us like that, not to mention climbing a wall Mommy had said not to." Rourke paused, then grinned. "Tomorrow, we wash my car. And you, Tory my sweet, will clean the interior."

Kat's muttered comment, "Some punishment. You two *love* washing your new car," had Tory giggling and Rourke winking over the little girl's head to her mother.

Early the next morning, Rourke eased into Kat's room. She'd said to wake her by nine. But how could he? Her worry over Tory and their three-hour stay at the hospital had taken their toll. He hadn't felt any too keen, himself. He suspected he'd never forget his feelings of helplessness as the doctor had set Tory's arm.

He loved Tory, but no way could he handle the lifetime of worry she'd give him. The childhood injuries. The growing-up. The dating. All those teenaged boys and their raging hormones. Thank God, he was Mr. Wrong and Kat had her sights set elsewhere.

A moment later, Rourke found himself beside Kat's bed, staring at her. Damn her! She could at least cover herself when sleeping.

Rourke knew he should walk away but couldn't. She was lying on her back, her rumpled sheet tossed to the side. The hem of her silk gown scrunched up near the apex of her thighs, exposing her long legs and the curve of her hip. Her long, sable hair covered one breast. His hand twitched.

"Rourke?" Kat whispered, her voice still groggy with sleep.

His throat clamped closed. "Yes." He winced at his hoarse whisper.

"What time is it?"

"Ten-thirty."

"You were supposed to get me up at nine!" Kat pushed her long, thick hair back off her face. "Why didn't you?"

"You went through an emotional wringer yesterday. It took a lot out of you. Don't worry, I've fed Tory and right now she's inspecting my car."

Rourke stood frozen at the foot of her bed, his eyes glued

to her long legs. The gown had inched up another notch and hid nothing. If forced to testify in court, he'd swear he hadn't looked. "Did you say something?"

"No, why?"

Spellbound, he watched Kat adjust her gown. He needed to leave. Now! Rourke started to back out of her room. He couldn't hear a thing over the pounding of his heart and the roar of blood rushing through his veins. Unable to tear his gaze from her legs, he tripped over one of her tennis shoes, caught himself, and stumbled. "I'll be outside with Tory," he mumbled as he shut the door.

Kat collapsed against her pillows and stared into space. What was going on? Here she lay in a sheer gown and no panties. And what happens? Rourke couldn't get out the door fast enough.

So much for her instincts. She'd completely misread what happened between them yesterday.

Well, to heck with him. After her success at B.B's, she no longer needed a teacher. She was ready to graduate and go hunting without her self-appointed chaperone.

Half an hour later, Kat popped the lid of her second diet cola and stared down at the aluminum. She never should have asked Rourke for his help. The man was impossible. Always had been and always would be. Pride and arrogance ruled him.

Kat gazed out the kitchen window and watched as he removed his shirt and threw it over the limb of the dogwood tree. Laughing at something Tory said, Rourke grabbed his soapy sponge from the bucket and waved it threateningly at her before turning back to his car.

Rourke's arm stretched over the roof of his sleek, black BMW. Kat swallowed hard at the fluid, rippling motion of the muscles in his bare back and shoulders. Rourke sparked dangerous, uncontrollable urges, urges she wanted to deny.

She wanted to be his car. To feel his fingers probing, searching, uncovering. . . . She wanted to feel his hands glide up and over her. She wanted him to pull her close to him and—*Stop!*

He's washing his car—not you!

Rourke walked toward the garage to retrieve the hose. Kat inhaled sharply. His smooth stride was lazy, yet predatory. "Lordy, he's magnificent," she murmured, fanning herself with the newspaper. "Double blast. Number six just crashed and burned. Kat, your problem is simple. You, my horny friend, need a man. Fast."

The last thing she could afford was to fall for a Number Nine control freak like Rourke. Lust would not derail her search for Mr. Right.

Images of Kat, of their kiss, tormented him. Ever since he agreed to Kat's outrageous proposal, Rourke had felt as if he were on a runaway train to hell. But if he jumped off, he'd lose what little control he had and learn the real meaning of hell.

"Rourke? Can I rinse the car?"

"Sure. Follow me with the hose." Rourke winked at Tory. "We'll finish faster if you rinse the soap off the car right after I wash it."

Tory picked up the hose. "Okie-dokie." She quickly rinsed the BMW's left rear hubcap. "Uncle Rourke?"

"Hmm?" After a few seconds of silence, Rourke glanced over at the little girl. With her brow puckered, she looked like a miniature Kat. "Tory, honey. You can ask me anything. You know that, don't you?"

"Uh-huh." Tory bit her lip as she looked down at her tennis shoe and kicked a rock. "If Mommy gets married again, the man will be my new daddy, won't he?"

"Yes." Seeing Tory's shoulders slump, Rourke squatted beside her and placed his hand on her shoulder. "Why, sweetheart? Has something happened that's worrying you?"

"Uh-huh." Tory paused to wipe her nose with the back of her hand. "I heard Mommy and Aunt Liz talking."

"Oh?" Leave it to his sister to be at the center of whatever was troubling Tory. "When did this happen?"

"Thursday," she answered softly, still looking at her feet. "I kinda, accidentally, picked up the phone and listened to them."

"And?"

Tory scuffed the toe of her sneaker on the ground.

"Mommy told Aunt Liz that she wants to start dating men, an' Aunt Liz said it was about time, an' she told Mommy it was time she forgot Daddy an' fell in love with a real man an' got married again, an' Mommy said she was workin' on it." Tory paused and took a deep breath.

"Mommy said she asked you to help her learn how to date an' meet some men an' you said okay just like Aunt Liz said you would. Did you?" she asked, looking up at him.

"Yes," Rourke answered in a soft, careful voice. Now it made sense. He'd suspected his sister was behind this insanity. Now he had proof! When he got his hands on her—

"But I want *you* to be my daddy. If you help Mommy date, she'll find somebody else, an' I want you for my daddy. I love you."

Rourke removed the hose from her limp hand, turned off the nozzle and laid it on the ground beside him. Carefully, he placed Tory's small, fragile hand in his much larger one. "Princess, I love you, too. I love you so much, sometimes just looking at you makes me want to burst from all the love inside. Nothing and no one will ever change that."

"You love Mommy, too."

"Yes I love her. I've loved her since I was just a little older than you. But it's a different kind of love."

Tory raised her face. "You love Mommy that special way!" she said with absolute certainty.

"That special way?" he repeated carefully.

"You know, like in the movies."

Rourke's brows drew together. "What movies, Tory?"

"Oh, you know. The mushy kind. Like on HBO or Showtime. I watch them at Kim's house. Mommy doesn't know," she whispered.

"Kim's mommy lets you watch mushy movies on cable at her house?"

"No, not her mommy! Kim's big brother. He was babysitting. Boy, was Kim's mommy mad when she found out. Alex got grounded for *two whole weeks!*"

Tory put her arms around Rourke's neck. He struggled to maintain a smile when her cast clunked him on the back of the head.

"I saw you making goo-goo eyes at Mommy. That's why I slipped and fell. So, if you love Mommy, why don't you marry her and be my daddy?"

Rourke looked away from the intense scrutiny of the six-year-old. Damn her eyes. They looked too much like Kat's. How was he going to get himself from this one? "Tory." He paused. "What you saw isn't what you think." He hoped the explanation didn't sound as lame to Tory as it did to him.

"No! It was mushy. Like on TV. And if you really loved us, you would marry Mommy and be my daddy."

"Sugar, there're different types of love. There's the love your mommy feels for you. There's the love she feels for her mom and dad, Aunt Liz, and me," he said placatingly. "And then, there's that special kind of love, the love a man and woman feel for each other."

Tory's green eyes narrowed in grim determination. "No! I saw you! You love Mommy the mushy way."

The little squirt wasn't listening to a word he said. Or, if she was, she wasn't buying it. Damn, now what did he say?

"Come on you two, lunch is ready."

Rourke exhaled in relief at Kat's timely call to the picnic table. Then he glanced at Tory. One look at her pushed out lower lip told him this recess was just that, a recess.

Kat watched Tory slow down as she entered the house, then turned back to Rourke. "You know you're grown up, Rourke, when you hear your parents' words coming out of your own mouth." Kat shook her head and bit into her sandwich.

"What words of wisdom have come full circle?"

Rourke's attempt to hide his amusement caused Kat to smile. He couldn't do it. It didn't work. It never did. The foolish man actually thought he kept a deadpan expression. Hah! His eyes gave him away every time. They turned slate gray when angry and a soft pewter when happy. She'd even heard via the bitch, Clarissa, they were a liquid silver color when—

Kat shook herself and forced a smile. "I just warned Tory to walk, not run. Talk about feeling like a fool. Here's a child who fell and broke her arm while walking along the ledge of a stone bridge like some tightrope walker, and I'm worried about her running too fast."

Rourke laughed. Not a soft, polite chuckle, but a full-bodied deep laugh. The kind a man gave when relaxed and enjoying himself. Kat felt her insides turn to mush. She grabbed her glass and took a sip of lemonade.

This was a disaster. He was a Number Nine, in caps. It had to stop. Now!

"I've decided I'm ready for a trial run on a real date." Kat patted his arm. "You've been very helpful. In fact, what you've done is above and beyond the call of duty. I mean, there aren't many men who'd have let me try out my kissing technique."

"Are you telling me those kisses were experiments?"

As Rourke's eyes changed to a frigid slate-gray, Kat swallowed hard. "Naturally. What else could they be?"

"What else could they be, indeed." Rourke slammed his lemonade down on the table, spilling his drink.

She reached for the napkins.

"I'll do it." Rourke snatched the stack of napkins and began mopping up the mess. "I told you I made the rules, not you. If you want practice, Katherine, I want to know it's practice."

Kat winced. Not good. He'd used her full name. "I'm sorry, Rourke. I never meant . . . What I mean is, how could I trust the response you gave if you'd known it was only an experiment? As it was, on a scale of one to ten, I figure I only scored a seven. But hey, that's better than the two's I was getting with Mark, isn't it?"

"For the record, you're a ten."

Kat sat up straight, grinning like a fool. She felt like she'd just won the lottery. Not the Pick Four or Lotto, but PowerBall when it got up in the nine digits. "Wow, a ten! Wow! Really?"

"Really."

At Rourke's less-than-enthusiastic response, Kat's smile dimmed. She reached out and touched his hand. "I couldn't have asked for a better teacher. The nightclub was an especially good idea. I never realized how many men were available."

"Kat—" Rourke stopped and lifted his gaze heavenward.

If Kat hadn't known better, she'd have sworn he was praying. "As I said, I'm ready to go out on my own."

"Has the kid doctor called?"

"Someone fresh out of diapers doesn't interest me. Although, he did ask," she said softly.

"I knew it. I just knew it," Rourke growled. He leaned forward and tipped her face towards his. "Men see you coming and know you're an easy mark. Naive. A few sweet words and next thing you know, you'll be flat on your back with your panties hanging from a lamp."

Kat jerked free. "I assume this is personal experience talking."

"Give me some credit. Even in high school I had more class than that."

She glared at him. He was too much. "Yeah, right. Good old Rourke's been around the block so many times he's worn a rut in the concrete. Women have fallen for him so often he's installed an air mattress at his front door. Why, all of his past lovers have formed a support group to break the habit. An—"

"Katherine, enough!"

"Darn right it is!" It was a good thing she'd never considered him for Mr. Right. How dare he say she was a naive incompetent! She'd show him.

"I've graduated, teach. Thanks for everything." Kat stood. "For the record, you're like the fisherman who's been fishing for twenty years and has gained only one year of experience." After one last glare, she spun and stalked toward the kitchen.

"My air mattress won't be here to catch you when you fall!"

Kat glanced back at Rourke. "Good thing, too. It's flat from all the usage."

CHAPTER FIVE

Peering through the peephole of her front door, Kat felt a shudder whip through her. Marvin Alcott wasn't a little paranoid, he was off the wall. He was wearing a raincoat on a cloudless day with the temperature hovering around eighty at seven in the evening.

Thank God, Tory was at Liz's. *Liz!* Kat shook her head. When would she ever learn not to trust her best friend's judgment in men?

Okay, so Marvin looked like a caricature of an FBI agent. Who cared? He was a date. She needed the experience, weird or not.

Pasting a smile on her face, Kat opened the door. "Marvin?"

Marvin slowly removed his sunglasses and nodded. He glanced in both directions, then sidled into the foyer. "You know my name?"

"Of course. Liz told me. She told you my name, didn't she?"

Marvin nodded. "You're Kat." He eased into the living room and made a circuit examining each light fixture. "Your lamps look clean."

"Thank you. I make it a point to dust the bulbs."

"But I haven't checked this out, yet. Can't be too careful," he whispered.

Kat stood dumbstruck as he crossed the room and started to dismantle her telephone. "You can put it together, again, can't you?" she croaked.

"No problem." In less time than it took to speed dial her folks in Florida, he'd reassembled the phone. Removing his trench coat, he tossed it over the back of the sofa. "One in a hundred homes is bugged and the owner doesn't know."

"No kidding? Where'd you read that?"

"*Soldier of Fortune.*"

Kat bit the inside of her cheek as the image of Marvin in military fatigues, crawling through enemy territory flashed in her mind. "Would you like a drink before we leave?" She strode over to the bar and poured herself a double Scotch. Neat.

Marvin stared at the bar, then at her, then back at the bar. "No, thanks. Decreases your reaction time and numbs your senses."

"Guess that's a *no.*" Kat took a gulp. "You learn that from *Soldier of Fortune,* too?"

"Nope, the Internet." He settled himself on the outer edge of the sofa.

Kat crossed the room and sat in a chair facing Marvin. "Liz says we're a lot alike. Both accountants. I'd love to know what other things we share in common."

"Why?" Marvin lifted the cushion next to him and inspected under it.

"Well, it's kind of customary for blind dates to talk and find out a little about each other. Isn't it?"

"Wouldn't know. Never been on one. Mother didn't approve."

"Mother?" Kat managed to swallow a groan.

"She died six months ago."

"Oh, I'm so sorry."

"It's been hard. I miss her very much." Marvin pulled a handkerchief from his jacket's breast pocket and mopped his eyes. "I don't have anyone to cook or sew for anymore. That's why Liz thought we might get along."

"Excuse me?"

Marvin lifted his teary gaze. "Both of us have lost someone recently."

"How thoughtful of Liz." Kat downed the rest of her drink in one gulp. *I'll kill her! This time I really, truly mean it!* With a slow, deliberate movement, she rose, returned to the bar and poured herself another drink. If there were ever a time to get sloshed, now was it. At least no one, especially her daughter who qualified as the McLean blabbermouth, was around to witness her humiliation.

She took a long sip. Spotting some napkins, her gaze widened. Why not? She turned and, dabbing her eyes, faced her date. "I'm sorry, Marvin," she said, her choked voice barely audible. "This talk about the loss of loved ones has brought back all of my pain. Do you mind if we cancel tonight?"

With her drink in one hand and napkin in the other, she walked to the door, dabbing at her mock tears.

Marvin nodded. "I knew it was too soon."

Kat had the door open before Marvin retrieved his trench coat. "Maybe another time, once we've accepted our losses."

"Maybe. I think I'll go put fresh flowers on Mother's grave."

"You do that." Kat moved aside and let him pass. "Watch for land mines," she said, then shut the door and raced for the phone. "She's dead meat! There's not a jury that'd convict me!" Kat muttered, punching the speed dial code for Liz's number. "What the hell did I ever do to make you hate me? And don't play innocent with me, Liz!"

"Are you okay?"

"I'm just hunky-dory." Kat sipped her drink. "I'm also getting not so quietly drunk."

"I'll be right over."

"Yeah, you do that." Kat slammed the receiver down and marched into the kitchen. Time to buy a *Soldier of Fortune*. It would have the perfect method of torture for interfering friends who screw up your life.

Amused, Kat moved behind the kitchen island as she watched Liz pace the floor. She enjoyed making her best friend squirm, loved seeing Liz on edge, unsure if she'd read Kat correctly.

There was a lot to be said for keeping people off-balance. She'd have to remember this around Rourke the next time he gave her a hard time.

"Why'd you set me up with Marvin?" Kat smiled at Liz's grimace and pulled a chopping knife from the wooden block. "Ignore the knife, Liz. You know I won't use it. Unless of course," Kat paused and ran her finger along the knife's razor edge, "your answers continue to displease me."

"Yeah, right. I'm shaking in my flip-flops."

Waving the knife in Liz's direction, Kat began slicing vegetables for her dinner. "You've talked a lot, Liz, but haven't said a thing. Bottom-line it. Why'd you saddle me with Marvin?" Kat set the knife down, walked around the island and sat down on one of the barstools. "Okay, I'm unarmed. Confession time. Is Marvin your accountant? Is that how you met him?"

Liz sat on the stool next to Kat and played with a basket of fruit. "Well, not exactly."

"Is he a patient?"

Liz lifted her head. "Kinda."

Kat groaned, leaned forward and pretended to beat her forehead on the oak island. "Why didn't I see this coming?"

"Honest, Kat. I thought Marvin was okay. He must have relapsed."

"Whatever." Kat glared at Liz. "Did you know he reads *Soldier of Fortune*?"

"A-*gain*? Damn! I thought I'd cured him of that." Liz grinned. "All things considered, it could have been worse. You could have actually gone out in public with him and Rourke might have seen you."

"Not funny! The truth, Liz, now!"

"Marvin was the best I could do on short notice, but I'll do better next time. Promise."

"There won't be a next time. From now on, I'll get my own dates." Kat smiled as Liz blanched.

"I've got to get home. See you tomorrow for a day of sun and fun."

As they headed toward the kitchen door, the phone rang. "Lordy, who could that be?"

"Not Rourke. He's at my house."

"Are you saying he knows my date was a bust?" Kat yelled.

"Of course not. I told the guys I had to get something from the store. Which is why I've got to leave."

Frowning, Kat answered the ringing phone. "Hello." At Liz's raised eyebrows, Kat mouthed, *Garrison*.

Kat sat up on her air cushion, squirted sunscreen on her legs and rubbed. "I accepted the date so I can get out from under Rourke's thumb. He's become a real pain. Stifling."

"Not to mention incredibly virile."

"Oh, *please*. Give me a break." Kat glared at Liz as she floated in the middle of her pool. "He's like an older brother."

Liz turned toward Kat and wagged her index finger. "Better be careful with your word choices. If you keep thinking about him as a brother, you could end up in an incestuous relationship."

Kat hit the water with the edge of her hand splashing Liz. "You're nuts." She slid off her raft and breaststroked to the side of Liz's pool. As she started to pull herself out of the water, she paused and slid down. She turned back to Liz. "You're matchmaking again, aren't you? Come on, admit it. That's why you talked me into asking Rourke for help!"

"Guilty as charged."

"Darn you! You're the worst matchmaker this side of Hades. Look what happened the last time you helped me. I married Mark." Kat swam to the stairs and climbed out. She faced Liz. "I'll do just fine on my own. I don't need your help or Rourke's."

"Did I hear my name?"

Startled, Kat pitched forward, landing a perfect belly flop. As she surfaced, she caught Liz's wink to her older brother and heard her ask, "Have you come to join us?"

"Not today. I'm meeting with a client in an hour."

Kat's eyes widened. "In jeans?"

"It's on his boat." Rourke grinned. "Where's Carl? He has to look over some papers before my meeting."

"The family room." Liz nodded her head toward the sliding glass doors. "He's watching *Beauty and the Beast* with the kids."

As Rourke bent down and grasped her hand, she inhaled his fresh scent. How was it possible for him to smell so delicious without a drop of after-shave?

"How's the dating game going?" he asked, pulling her out of the water.

She hated his smug smirk. Boy, was he in for a surprise. "Great. Guess who I'm going to the Kennedy Center Benefit with?" she said, trying to gain her balance.

"Okay, I give. Who?"

"Garrison."

"Garrison? My cousin, Garrison Mitchell?" Rourke asked in a low voice.

Grinning, Kat nodded. Rourke released her hand. She flopped backward and landed bottom first. Seconds later, she surfaced, sputtering. Shoving her hair out of her eyes, she glared up at Rourke.

Kat swam to the stairs and climbed out of the pool. She should have kept her mouth shut and shown up at the benefit on Garrison's arm. Lesson learned: to maintain thinking skills, stay out of sniffing range of Rourke.

Rourke glowered down at Liz, then turned back to Kat. "I wouldn't suggest starting your dating career with him."

"I'm not. I've had several dates. Why, just last night I had a date with a wonderful man. A real homebody. And real protective, too." Kat grabbed her towel and began to pat herself dry. "He wants to make sure everything around the woman in his life's secure."

Kat's gaze met Liz's. If Liz uttered one word, or let loose with her barely contained laughter, next time she'd *use* the knife. Kat turned and poked Rourke in the chest. "You should be happy, your lessons are paying off!"

"I am. But you're searching for Mr. Right, and Garrison isn't the man for you."

According to Liz, Garrison only wanted a woman's mystery. Once the puzzle was solved, he moved on. However, she'd be darned if she'd admit Garrison was Mr. Wrong to "Rourke-The-Number-Nine." Kat shrugged. "Too bad. He's my date for the benefit Saturday night."

"Yes, but the question is why. It's out of character for him to call at the last minute." Rourke glanced at an innocent-looking Liz floating in the middle of the pool and inhaled sharply.

Liz rolled onto her stomach and paddled to the pool's

side. "Don't look my way, bro. Garrison and Kat were over here this past Wednesday and hit it off."

"What's the matter, Rourke? Think I can't attract men on my own?"

"Of course not. It's just—"

"You don't approve."

Liz stepped between Kat and Rourke. "You're adults, act like it."

"Butt out, Liz," Rourke snarled.

"Yeah." Kat shot Liz a look that had her backing away from them. "As I said, Garrison isn't my first date. I've been out three times."

"Your dates with me don't count."

"Agreed." Kat grinned.

Rourke frowned. "What three dates?"

"Last night's and the two with Bruce Chambers." Kat stepped back and swallowed hard. The muscle in Rourke's jaw ticked. His eyes turned a frigid slate. "Don't worry, he doesn't meet any of my criteria."

Rourke's arm circled Kat's wrist. "Back up. When did you go out with Bruce Chambers?"

"When do you think? This past week. And I did just fine without your air mattress for fall-back." Kat tried to think of anything but Rourke. His grip loosened and his fingers began to caress the inside of her wrist. Her skin burned. She was going up in flames. *Get away before you make a fool of yourself and attack him.*

"Give him the good news about Clarissa, Liz. That should cheer him up."

"Clarissa? What the hell's she got to do with this?"

Kat cocked her head and stared up at him in disbelief. The crumb! The two-timing sleaze! Making love to her hand, clouding her mind with his scent when all the while he'd taken back up with the screech owl. No more forgetting he was Mr. Wrong.

"I only know what Liz told me." Kat shot her friend a furious glare. "I have to go. Tory's waiting." Kat jerked free and bolted for the house.

"Remind me! That's rich." Rourke jammed his hands in his pants pockets to keep from throttling his sister. "Until this moment, I didn't know anything about the benefit!"

"Posh." Liz waved her hand. "You love the opera. It's going to be *Carmen*."

"Stop the delaying tactics. You're out of order on this, Liz." Rourke grasped her shoulders and gave her a sharp shake. "Today's the first I've heard of the benefit, or Clarissa."

"She said sitting with all of us was your decision. I mean, you two have gotten back together again, haven't you?"

"Excuse me? Are you telling me Clarissa is my date for the evening?"

"According to Clarissa, yes." Liz pulled free, walked over to a lounge chair and stretched out. "The Bitch said because the two of you had just gotten back together, she couldn't change the location of her seat for the opera. But for me not to worry, as if I would. She's been able to switch with someone for the dinner afterwards." Liz popped the tab on a cola. "I'm not your parole officer, big brother, and you don't file reports with me. So when a female announces she's your woman, and she *was* once on your arm, who am I to argue?"

"This keeps getting better and better. I'm stuck with Clarissa and Kat gets her dream date with Garrison." Rourke pinched the bridge of his nose.

"She doesn't need your censure or approval, Rourke. And if you aren't careful, you'll shove her right into his arms."

Rourke stifled a groan. *And his bed.*

"If it'll make you feel better, just remember you'll be there to chaperone," Liz said sweetly. She grabbed his hand. "It's important Kat knows you're in her corner, available for support if she needs it. She isn't ready for someone as dynamic and forceful as Garrison."

"Dynamic? Forceful?"

"Yup. Dynamic and forceful. And I've warned her the word is he's a great lover. But Kat's not ready for the big leagues yet, so having you there will give her some much needed confidence."

Rourke stood stock-still. A great lover! Not ready for the big leagues yet? What did that make him, the farm team? He didn't know whether to laugh or be insulted.

For a shrink, Liz was sometimes incredibly stupid. The last thing Kat needed, right now, was a relationship with their cousin. Rourke couldn't remember being this angry with Liz since she'd introduced Kat to Mark. Just whose side was his sister on? First, she promoted Kat and Mark's romance. Now, she was pushing Garrison.

"I've got to go." Rourke stalked to his BMW, got in, threw it in gear, and peeled out of Liz's driveway. He knew where to lay this mess and Liz would pay. He'd enjoy every minute. He'd make sure torture was long and slow. It'd come when she least expected it. Oh, yes, she'd pay. Big time.

CHAPTER SIX

Kat tilted her head and slid her hands down the sides of her black, form-fitting gown. The enormity of her accomplishment hit her. In only a few weeks, she'd managed to turn a drab, nondescript accountant into a vibrant, self-assured woman.

For the first time in her life, she appreciated the nickname Rourke saddled her with so long ago. From this moment forward, she would remind herself she was no longer an ordinary house cat, but Kat—sleek, long-limbed, and sexy. She swore insecurity would no longer plague her, or rule her decisions.

She pulled her new chin-length hair off her left side and secured it with a black-enamel, rhinestone-encrusted comb. Standing back, she surveyed the results. Yes, the soft, feminine look pleased her. She hoped Rourke agreed.

Where had that come from? Rourke was Mr. Wrong!

A tube of Blush Pink lipstick was discarded. "No. No more." She threw it into the wastebasket. Grabbing one of her new shades, she applied Firelight Red to her lips. "You want red-light district, you've got it."

She loved the Kennedy Center. As she and Garrison approached The Grand Foyer, Kat paused. Before her lay a magnificent mirrored room patterned after the Galerie des Glaces in Versailles. The extraordinary chandeliers from Sweden only added to the room's beauty and turned the Hall of Mirrors into a magical wonderland.

After the opera, this elegant room would be the setting for

the benefit's dinner and dance.

The theater exuded beauty, elegance, and refinement. Walking down the aisle to her seat under the starburst chandelier, she felt like an enchanted princess.

"Oh good, we're all sitting together," Kat said when she reached their row and saw Liz, Carl, and Rourke. She glanced around. "Where's Clarissa? I'd so looked forward to her joining us."

"Oh, I know you did," Liz said. "Have no fear, she'll be at our table after the opera. Rourke!" Liz swatted her brother with a rolled up program. "Aren't you going to say hello to Kat and Garrison?"

Rourke snapped his program closed. "Sorry," he mumbled. "Hi." He glanced up. Relief coursed through him. Black velvet covered her from collarbone to toe.

Then, he spotted the black lace that started just beneath her boobs and ended at her hip. Worse, was the slit from floor to mid-thigh! The damned gown was premeditated seduction, and there was no way she could plea-bargain it.

Kat moved forward. Rourke's mouth went dry. Her walk was an advertisement for raw sex. Men who saw her would be after her like a pack of bloodhounds with Garrison leading the race.

"Hi, guys." Garrison nodded to his cousins.

Rourke's hand tightened around his program. What did Kat think she was doing, slanting Garrison that come-an'-get-it look?

Kat leaned over and kissed Rourke's cheek. "Welcome back, Mr. Kotter," she whispered with a smile.

Mr. Kotter, my ass! Grim determination filled him. No one, not his cousin, nor that security-minded homebody was going to have Kat. She'd been hurt once, he wouldn't let it happen, again.

★ ★ ★ ★ ★

Kat hadn't missed Rourke's brief flash of disapproval. But, tonight, she didn't care. Whatever his problem, she wasn't going to let it ruin her evening.

Easier said than done, Kat thought. For the last fifty minutes, she'd felt Rourke's arctic gaze on her, freezing, yet burning her. It had taken all her strength to sit still and not squirm.

As the curtains closed for intermission, Kat exhaled in relief. She leaned over and whispered to Garrison, "I'll be back in a few minutes." She eased out of her seat and slipped from the theater.

Once safely in the ladies' room, she fell unceremoniously onto the small vanity chair and stared at her reflection. "Make-up might have made you more attractive to men, but it sure didn't make you any smarter."

"Once a sow's ear, always a sow's ear?"

Kat stiffened. Clarissa. Kat glanced at the svelte blonde's reflection. "It takes a pig to know one." She refused to allow the ice-queen to unnerve her. If she could match Clarissa's cool delivery, Kat knew she could handle any situation.

"My, aren't we quick this evening," Clarissa said.

"Just practicing my lines," Kat returned with a firm smile.

"Mmm," Clarissa purred. "I suppose one must do that if she's inexperienced. Keep trying, dear." With a chuckle, she glided out of the women's lounge.

Kat turned back to the mirror. "You did okay." After reapplying her red lipstick, she rose from the chair. "Remember, retreat is not an option."

As she emerged from the bathroom, Kat saw Rourke advancing toward her. She paused. Head up, she moved past him.

His hand snaked out and snagged her arm. Rourke bent

down, his lips brushed her ear. "Ignoring your teacher, Kat? Better show some respect, or you'll get detention."

The contact sent electricity shooting up her arm. She wished he'd stop touching her. She couldn't think with his fingers stroking her arm. From the gleam in his eyes, she knew he knew her pulse had kicked into overdrive. "But, Rourke, how can I have detention when I've already graduated."

"Ouch!" He winced. "In other words, you don't need me to coach you any more on re-entering the *Meat Market*."

"Bingo!" Kat jerked free of his grasp. Darn him, why was he doing this? Why was he using the low tone that sent shivers of desire racing along every nerve? In this case, retreat was the only option. Turning, she raced back to Garrison.

"You okay?" Garrison asked as Kat settled herself in her seat.

"Yes." She paused as Rourke eased past her. "Sorry I was delayed. Too many hens in the same chicken coop."

The opera's second half went unnoticed as Kat lectured herself. *Remember, you're Kat the sleek, not the common. It'll take more than "Number Nine" and a bitchy blonde to throw you off course.*

Garrison leaned over. "The opera's over, Kat. Time to go." He took her hand and helped her from her seat.

"Don't worry. I know where our table is," Garrison said, smoothly taking Kat's arm and escorting her through the crowd.

"I'm glad someone does," Rourke muttered.

"Liz told me earlier where we were sitting. We're next to the windows and across from the bust of Kennedy. I'm surprised she didn't tell you, too, Rourke."

"I talk more to the pizza man than my sister." He's right,

Rourke fumed, trailing behind Kat and Garrison. Liz had been behind the date. He'd force his sister into full disclosure before this evening was over.

Fifteen minutes later, Rourke's hands clenched into tight fists. Garrison's hand rested on Kat's midriff and his thumb was just under her breast. Rourke knew Garrison was up to his old game of one-upmanship. When he grinned and slid a hungry gaze over Kat, Rourke flexed his fingers and eased over to his cousin's side. "If it's war you want, it's war you'll get. Back off."

"This ain't college, cuz. Kat's a big girl, now. She doesn't need your protection."

A sigh escaped as her gaze drifted over the assembled crowd. Kat couldn't believe it. She'd actually met people she read about in the *Washington Post*'s "Style Section." Not to mention a number of eligible bachelors! It looked as if finding a date wasn't going to be difficult. Mr. Right had to be here, somewhere. So why wasn't she excited about the prospect?

"I never thought I'd get here."

Clarissa!

"Well, Katherine, did you memorize all your lines?" Clarissa drawled.

"I believe in ad-libbing."

"I assume warm and fuzzy is out this evening," Garrison said in a low whisper.

Kat nodded. "Clarissa just fired a warning shot over my bow. She enjoys toying with her victims before closing in for the verbal kill." She glanced at Clarissa and spotted a small smirk playing at the corner of the woman's mouth. "And I do believe, she's getting ready for her next salvo."

"I take it she's not one of your favorite people," Garrison said.

"I'd rather eat fried worms than spend an evening in her company."

At Garrison's shout of laugher, Clarissa returned her ice-filled glare to Kat. "It takes more than poise to get and keep a man at home, doesn't it, dear?"

Rourke eased into his chair. "When you find the secret you'll share it, won't you, Clarissa?"

"Rourke, darling, you're such a tease. You'll make these people think I haven't found the answer." Clarissa's long fingernail traced his jaw.

The muscle in his jaw tightened. "If you want to stay at this table, I suggest you can it. Now!"

"Rourke, you missed it. Katherine's surprised me. I didn't realize she had a sense of humor. In fact, she's known as something of a drone. Both in and out of—"

"Time to get out the litter box," Liz said, brightly.

Garrison leaned over and whispered in Kat's ear, "Okay, let's have it. What happened between you two?"

Kat tried to ignore Rourke's smoldering gaze, Liz's twinkling eyes, and Clarissa's glare of retribution. "Later. After we eat," Kat whispered, looking down at her salad.

She wished Garrison's touch made her melt into a puddle of wax the way Rourke's did. What was wrong with her? She and Rourke had known each other for twenty-seven years. Why after all these years, had she become aware of him as a man, not just the older brother of her best friend?

Two hours later, Garrison set his dessert fork down, smiled at his table companions and stood. "If you all don't mind, Kat and I want to dance for awhile. Work off the excellent meal," he said, helping Kat out of her chair. As they walked away, he said, "Okay, let's have it. What happened?"

"What are you talking about?"

"Clarissa, what else?"

"Do you have to ruin my digestion? It was hard enough looking at her, do we have to talk about her too?"

"You promised to tell me the story. I already know you called her the 'screech owl from hell.' As I recall, Liz had a field day with it. And when they broke up, Rourke slipped and said she sounded like one."

Garrison cocked his head to the side. "From the black looks she's shot your way, I'd say, whether or not the woman knows you're responsible for the name, she hates you. So give."

"You're right. It doesn't have anything to do with a nickname. It dates back to the time Clarissa and Rourke were still an item." Kat grinned.

"It started the night I went into labor with Tory—two weeks early. I couldn't reach a soul. My parents and the Hawthornes were all up at our cabin. And Liz, my Lamaze coach, was in Chicago attending a conference. So, I called the only person I could think of, Rourke."

Kat paused, remembering that night in detail. Including why she wasn't home with her husband. Mark had claimed since he had to make repeated trips to Europe during the last months of her pregnancy, he'd feel better if she were home with her family. She'd believed him. So she'd returned to McLean, Virginia. Only later did she learn the truth, he'd hated looking at her swollen belly.

"Okay, but what's that have to do with Clarissa?"

At Garrison's deep voice Kat shook her head and smiled. "Honest, never in my wildest imagination did I expect to interrupt anything. Who would? After all, it was five in the morning."

"Ah, true stamina runs in our family."

"So it seems." Kat's voice dropped even lower. "Apparently, I called right at the crucial moment and Rourke left her

. . . shall we say . . . unfulfilled. Clarissa was furious and said some things she shouldn't have and they broke up because of it."

"Clarissa has a reputation for keeping score."

"Yes, I know." Kat wished he'd loosen his hold. She hated being held tightly by men. It frightened her. Not that she'd ever admit that. So why did she feel alive, every cell tingling with anticipation, whenever Rourke touched her, held her?

She had to stop these fantasies. They were ridiculous and getting out of hand. Rourke had been like an older brother most of her life, offering help and advice whether she wanted it or not. If she didn't rein in her desires, she'd lose a life-long friend and her job.

"From what I've heard, Clarissa enjoys her revenge," Garrison said, snapping Kat back to reality.

Revenge was the perfect, bloodthirsty word, Kat thought. "Oh, she had her revenge. But that's another story." She thought back to her husband Mark's betrayal. That was one humiliation she never planned to share. Not with Garrison, or Liz, or even Rourke.

The evening was in close competition for the worst night in Rourke's memory. He watched Kat float past in Garrison's arms. Did she think he was made of stone? He'd watched her touch Garrison's arm and laugh and whisper. He'd endured seeing them dance so close a piece of paper couldn't fit between them. Embarrassment be damned, if the music hadn't stopped, he'd have stormed out there and separated them.

He glanced at his sister seated next to him. This was all Liz's fault. If they'd been alone, he'd have let her have it. Unfortunately, Clarissa was still at the table. Thankfully, she was talking to a friend.

"Stop glaring at me, Rourke," Liz said in a soft voice.

"Me? Glaring at you? Why would I do that, have you done something to deserve it?"

"Carl, tell him to behave. Jason Barrington's headed this way," Liz said. "Do something. Kat'll be here in a minute."

Great. Just great. When he thought things couldn't get worse, who shows up? The current Romeo of Capitol Hill, the wealthy and handsome Jason Barrington. One of *The Washingtonian*'s ten most eligible bachelors.

As she reached the table, Kat smiled in recognition. Jason lifted her hand to his lips. "Hello, Darlin'. It's good to see you, again."

The word *again* reverberated through Rourke's skull. He glanced at Carl. His brother-in-law rolled his eyes heavenward.

"Ah, they're playing some slow songs," Jason said, winking at Kat. He turned toward Garrison. "You don't mind if Kat and I have this dance, do you?"

"It's up to the lady in question."

At Kat's nod, Jason held out his hand for hers.

The moment they'd disappeared into the swirling maze of people, Rourke drilled his cousin a warning look. "Would you take Clarissa for a spin, Garrison? I need to talk with Liz for a few minutes—privately." Years of training helped him keep a conversational tone while under the table his left hand held Liz's thigh in a pincer grip.

"It'll be my pleasure. Come along, my dear." Garrison held out his hand to a pouting Clarissa. "I'm really a much better dancer than Rourke. Even Mrs. Pierson used to say so. But, no doubt, you remember our dance class and how great I was."

Once Clarissa and Garrison were safely out of earshot, Liz said, "Let go of my leg or lose a testicle."

Rourke released Liz. "What's going on?"

"I could ask you the same thing!" she exclaimed. "How could you let that shark near Kat?"

"Liz." Rourke's voice held a note of warning. "Jason is many things, but a shark isn't one of them."

"Pond scum has more honor than that Great White. Carl, educate your partner about that playboy dancing with Kat. He uses women. He'll break her heart."

Carl's response consisted of an elegantly raised eyebrow and an inelegant snort.

"Thanks, Carl," Rourke said. "I couldn't have said it better, myself. Now, stop trying to change the subject and answer my question. Why did you set Kat up with Garrison, especially knowing *his* reputation?"

"I—I didn't."

At Rourke's look of disgust, Liz flinched.

"Well, maybe I did. But it isn't like it's a real date." Liz glared at Rourke. "At least Garrison's family and won't use or hurt her like Jason. Besides, he's in it just to see your reaction."

"Liz," Rourke sighed, momentarily closing his eyes, "are you trying to ruin my life?"

"No," she answered in a small voice. "Don't you see—"

"Give it a rest. You had no business getting Garrison involved."

"Wrong, brother dear. Kat met Jason after you left our house Sunday and has been out with him."

Rourke sat in stunned silence, unable to comprehend and process what Liz was telling him.

"Carl and I gave a small dinner party that included Kat. I asked you, too, but your nose was still out of joint over Bruce Chambers. Jason took one look and moved in for the kill, teeth bared. Have you noticed how he has shark's eyes?"

"Liz!" Rourke expelled a sigh of frustration. When she

wanted to, his sister could make Edith Bunker look like a cut-to-the-chase-storyteller.

"Okay, okay. Since their first date, he's been calling Kat nightly. I was desperate, and you weren't an option." Liz touched Rourke's face. "You know how naive Kat is. I had to phone Garrison. I figured she would be safe with him. He's family."

Rourke dropped all pretense at calm and rational thought. One word burned in his mind, *traitor*. "You've lost your mind. Have you forgotten Garrison's history with women, or with me?"

"No. No. And no. Jeez, how dumb do you think I am? Garrison isn't eighteen. And he isn't going to use Kat as a prize in a game of one-upsmanship with you. Tell him, Carl. Tell him how it's different, now."

"I'm not going there." Carl sat back in his chair.

"Your support is under-whelming," Liz snapped.

"Leave Carl alone, and butt out of Kat's love life. She's an adult and perfectly capable of handling herself without help."

"Yeah, well, can't you?"

Rourke leveled a piercing glare. "I'm warning you, Liz. Stop meddling."

"Well, if you're going to get nasty about it, I won't. I only wanted Kat to be happy."

"For a shrink you sometimes show abysmal judgment." Rourke shook his head.

Hearing her husband snicker, Liz turned on him. "Oh, shut up, turncoat." Liz looked back at Rourke. "Listen, I thought if Garrison got involved, I could help nudge things along a little bit. You know, get past your paralysis where Kat's concerned."

Rourke grimaced. Liz was at her most dangerous when trying to help family and friends. He didn't know why he was surprised. Her fingerprints had covered this disaster from the beginning. "Oh, God, you've been matchmaking!"

"Just a little. But you're ruining everything. You've got to stop thinking of Kat as off limits because she's my best friend. And while I'm on the subject, why don't you start treating her like an adult?"

"What the hell are you talking about?"

"Your continual hovering and disapproval drives her crazy. I only wanted to help, Rourke. Honest."

With a harsh sigh, he looked at his sister. "I want your word of honor—what's left of it—that you'll butt out of Kat's and my love lives." Rourke didn't trust her hesitation. She was worse than any attorney. He could see the wheels turning as Liz weighed each word. If he didn't get her blanket promise now, she'd find a loophole and wiggle free. "Your promise, Liz, now!"

"Do you want me to swear on the family Bible?"

A surge of satisfaction roared through Rourke as Liz winced under one of his patented stares.

"Oh, all right, I promise. If you think you understand women, go ahead. Feel free to continue screwing up."

"Me? Screw up? You forget whom you're talking to. Now, if you'll excuse me, I'll go rescue Kat."

"Sorry Romeo, but it doesn't look like anyone needs rescuing. Least of all Kat. She's already left with a mouthful of canary."

Rourke searched the dance floor for her. *Where the hell was she?* His gaze narrowed. *And where was the slick and polished Mr. Barrington?* With balled fists shoved into his tuxedo trousers, he stood. "They're here somewhere, and I'll find them."

"Better watch how you handle this, or any good you could do helping Kat build her self-confidence and dating will be shot. That is, unless you're willing to admit you're interested in more than teaching her."

"I'm not." Rourke glared down at his seated sister. "I'm involved in this insane . . . whatever . . . because you and Kat are friends."

"In that case, remember this and remember it well: Kat doesn't want a vigilante arriving on the scene to rescue her. Nor will she appreciate the caveman routine. You know, beat your opponent over the head with a club and haul the woman off to your cave by her hair."

Rourke withdrew his hands from his slacks and stood, flexing them at his side. "I've always been a Southern gentleman, Liz. The caveman act isn't part of my repertoire. Against my better judgement, I got sucked into this business because I don't want to see Kat get hurt."

"At least we agree on something. Just be sure you don't hurt her, Rourke. Because whether you want to believe it or not, your words cut deeper than anyone else's, including Clarissa's."

"Me?"

"Yes, you."

Rourke frowned. Damn Liz, why'd she have to be right? Almost from the first time he'd met Kat, his sharp words seemed to pierce her in some way. He nodded to Liz and strode to the edge of the dance floor.

Not spotting Kat and Jason dancing, Rourke turned and studied the room's corners and deep shadows. Finally, he spotted them. Sherlock Holmes would have been proud. There they stood, hiding in plain sight, in front of the wall of mirrors.

Rourke shook his head. Being a teacher wasn't easy. Especially when his student kept ad-libbing.

The evening was a success. Kat looked up at Jason, real-

izing he really was a terrific-looking example of the male spe-
cies. He fit every one of her list's criteria. He was tall, blond,
and had the deepest blue eyes she'd ever seen. They reminded her of the blue from a cavalry uniform jacket.

Yet for some reason she didn't feel the fireworks she
should. Kat froze. Her instincts at war with her intellect.

He was reputed to be a ladies' man. A man who loved
women and whom women loved in return. Maybe she
wouldn't be the one to make him settle down, but it would
sure be fun trying. Besides, who knew what the future held?
For the moment, he was the only man she'd met whom she
could in all honesty say matched her list for Mr. Right perfectly.

"You're a beautiful woman, Kat. I have to ask you if you'd
do me the honor of going to the Eastern Shore with me before
the summer's over?"

"I'm not sure, Jason." She hesitated. "If you're still interested in a few weeks, could you ask then? At the moment, the
firm's in the middle of a divorce case, and I can guarantee
Rourke wouldn't appreciate my request for vacation time."

"Of course." Jason smiled.

Kat stared at the straight and incredibly white teeth. The
man was too perfect to be real. Of course, it was always possible he came up short where it mattered. Her gaze slipped
down then flew back to his face. Unless he used socks to pad
himself, it seemed nature had also bestowed him well below
the belt.

"Kat. Jason. I wondered where the two of you could have
gone."

"Hard to miss us standing over here in front of a bunch of
mirrors." Kat looked up at Rourke with irritation. The man
was insufferable. First, he'd caught her wrist when she'd
come out of the ladies' room, spewing all that teacher crap.

Now this. "Why don't you go back to the table like a nice little 'Do-Bee' and ask Clarissa, *your date,* for a dance."

Jason winked at Kat, and she watched to see if Rourke caught the move. From his expression, she didn't think so. He was intent on her face and most of the rest of her.

"Clarissa's doing just fine. I wonder if you can say the same?"

Jason stepped in front of Kat. "Are you suggesting that I, in any way, may be harming Kat?"

"No, but now that you mention it . . ."

"How about if the three of us get a glass of wine and toast one another? The Merlot they're serving is especially smooth for such a large crowd. Obviously Californian." Kat pivoted, and started to walk back toward her table.

Jason whistled. "Somehow, until just this second, I missed how daring the back of that dress is. It's just begging for a hand to slip right inside."

Kat turned and winked.

Rourke's fists clinched. Liz was right. He was paralyzed when it came to Kat. He'd fooled himself into thinking he'd gone along with her ridiculous request because of friendship, but the truth was his feelings were anything but friendly or altruistic. He wanted her. The only question was what was he going to do about it?

With a fixed smile, he clapped his hand on Jason's shoulder and squeezed. "You don't mind if I steal Kat, do you, Jason?"

"Only for tonight. I'll call you, Kat."

Rourke pulled Kat into his arms. He ignored the look of irritation she shot him and gave her a lazy smile.

"Rourke, you were very rude."

"Sue me. He's a user. Don't trust him, Kat. Relax, sweetheart, we're dancing, not fighting." He enjoyed the feel of her warm, lithe body melt against his. Her delicate scent played havoc with his common sense. "I love your perfume."

Kat snuggled closer. "I'm not wearing any."

All these years he'd thought she wore perfume. He shook his head at his stupidity. One would think, after having searched for that elusive scent and never finding it, he'd have realized it was Kat, her essence, he loved smelling.

"Tonight's been a fantasy come true," she murmured, her tone soft and dreamy as they waltzed around the floor. "And I'm really free. To dress how I want. To talk to men. To be the woman I've always longed to be."

Rourke pulled Kat flush against him. Damn, what if Liz was right? What if he'd waited too long?

Kat lifted her head from his shoulders. "Hasn't it been a wonderful night?"

Rourke looked down into her expectant eyes. "Yes," he said, his breath brushing her lips. "Definitely a night to remember."

CHAPTER SEVEN

Rourke exited the elevator and, pausing before a pair of large, mahogany doors, cringed. Tuesday and he was no closer to resolving the predicament of how to approach Kat than he'd been Saturday night.

Damn! When had his life become this complicated? The moment he'd crossed the boundary of friendship.

Squaring his shoulders, he entered his firm's outer reception room. As he approached his secretary's desk, Rourke glanced at Kat's office.

"If you're looking for Kat, she's out to lunch," Grace said.

"Out for lunch?" Rourke's alarm bells pealed at the same volume as when confronting unexpected and unwanted testimony. "Kat never goes out for lunch."

"True . . . but that was before TBH came on the scene."

"TBH?"

"Tall, blond hunk," she said with her hand patting her heart.

"Did this blond hunk happen to have a name?"

"Jason. He showed up yesterday, bearing two dozen red roses, and swept her away for a *long* lunch," Grace sighed. "You know, of course, red flowers mean love and passion. If yesterday was any indication, I wouldn't expect her back before one-thirty at the earliest, probably closer to two. Kat has all the luck," Grace murmured.

Rourke clenched his teeth so hard he was surprised one of his crowns didn't shatter under the pressure. "Have Ms.

Snow come to my office with the Michels file as soon as she returns."

"Since you didn't say anything to the contrary, Kat didn't think you'd need her." Grace glanced up from her computer screen. "She left the Michels file with all her findings on your desk."

"I see." Rourke took a deep breath and slowly exhaled. "Did she leave a contact number?"

"No. Why?"

"Let me know when she gets back." Rourke stalked into his office and carefully shut his door.

Jason!

Why did it have to be Jason? Rourke pressed a hand against the door. Kat should have kicked him in the balls. It'd have been cleaner and a helluva a lot less painful.

Jason opened the outside door of Kat's office building. "Thank you for the lovely lunch." Kat walked ahead of him to the elevators and punched the UP button. "The restaurant was beautiful. What I could see of it, that is. A bit dim for the middle of the afternoon, don't you think?"

Jason laughed. "I thought you'd enjoy eating where all the politicians take their lovers. You'd be surprised, even some of the more respectable names in Congress have a skeleton or two in their closets."

"That doesn't surprise me. Remember, I work for a divorce lawyer."

"I hope working for Rourke hasn't jaded you about marriage."

Kat moved to the side as they entered the empty elevator. "Of course not." She grinned up at him. "I'm looking forward to remarrying. To the right person, naturally." Kat sighed. "I'm looking for someone special. He has to like kids, and well, be suitable. An affair wouldn't suit me."

She glanced up at Jason's face and felt her cheeks burn. "Jason, I want to go out with a man and feel as free as a bird, but I don't want to make a nest without a ring. I want to remember what it's like to be pampered. I want to know my date enjoys my company as an intellectual equal. Then, I can naturally grow into a more intimate relationship. But not until then."

Kat bit her lip as Rourke's face flashed in front of her. Wasn't that the way he treated her? Yet, here she was with Jason.

Stop it, she ordered herself. Rourke didn't fit the criteria. No matter how attracted she might be to him, she refused to let her hormones dictate her future. She had more to consider than just herself. There was Tory . . .

"Don't you agree?"

Kat stared up at Jason in confusion. "Agree?"

"That I have been the perfect gentleman. I don't intend to do otherwise, until you say you want me to."

"Thank you, Jason. You're going to be a great husband and father one of these days."

"Ouch—what a comment."

Kat laughed at Jason's feigned injury.

"Those words are the kiss of death on a relationship. Are you telling me you don't find me attractive?"

"On the contrary," she denied. "You're very attractive. I saw a dozen sets of feminine eyes trained on you when we walked into that restaurant."

"That's not what I asked." Jason picked up her hand and gazed into her eyes. "Do *you* find me attractive?"

"Of c-course." Kat tripped over the words and winced at the amusement in Jason's eyes.

"In that case, I suppose you don't mind joining me for dinner?"

"I'd love to." Kat wished she felt excited about the prospect. Who was she kidding? Her idea of attractive was Rourke, and that was an image she had to dispel soon—at any cost.

Rourke motioned her to the leather wingback chair vacated by Lillian Michels. "Have a seat, Katherine," he said, then escorted Lillian to the outer office.

Kat sat bolt upright, her back rigid, her knees and ankles touching. Trouble was coming. He'd used her full name *again*.

She watched him return to the chair behind his desk and sit down. Leaning forward, he rested his elbows on the table and steepled his fingers. She bit the inside of her cheek. He'd probably kill her if she laughed, but darn, he looked just like her Dad did when working himself up for a lecture.

He could sit there like a sphinx for the next year for all she cared. She'd be dogged if she'd break the silence first. A small smile wanted to break free as she remembered Liz's lecture. Why the heck not?

Leaning back in the chair, Kat relaxed, adjusted her short, straight skirt an inch higher and crossed her legs. Satisfaction filled her as Rourke's gaze dropped to her exposed thigh and watched her swing her right leg with her high-heel dangling from her foot.

"We charge clients by the hour," he said, his voice hoarse, raspy. He shook his head, cleared his throat and raised his gaze to hers. "They have every right to expect us to be here as scheduled. Their time is as valuable as ours."

"And?" Hmm, maybe she was pushing the envelope. She didn't like Rourke's white-knuckled fists, and she sure didn't like that telltale tick of his jaw muscle.

"I suppose a two-hour lunch is a little long. Even if it happens only once or twice a year." Kat tapped her finger against her lips, then shrugged. "Jason's such good company I lost track of time. Sorry."

"You should be. I expected you here."

"Come off it, Rourke. I never attend client meetings."

"I wanted you at this one."

"I'm not a mind reader. I followed standard procedures and left the case file and all my findings in the middle of your desk."

"If you're ever late to a client meeting again because of a *personal* lunch date, Grace will clean out your desk for you."

Kat returned Rourke's stony expression. Who did he think he was kidding? This had nothing to do with work and everything to do with Jason Barrington. It was time Rourke learned a long over-due lesson. And she was just the Kat to shred his damned arrogant, dictator hide.

"Given your dissatisfaction with my work habits, you have my two weeks notice." She stood and smoothed her skirt over her hips. "Excuse me. I have to go call Bruce Chambers and let him know I'll be taking up his job offer."

Swearing softly, Rourke surged to his feet. "I never said I wanted you to leave! That's the last thing I want!"

Exhilaration filled Kat. She'd broken through his tightly leashed control and made him sweat. Kat advanced, rested her hands on his desk and leaned forward. "Really? I can't think of one reason why I shouldn't think you want to fire me."

Laughter threatened to erupt. Rourke's mind seemed to have momentarily shut down. She snapped her fingers in front of his face, shocking him out of his daze.

"I don't want you to quit. That's the last thing I want. It was a simple warning, nothing more."

Kat snorted. So much for Rourke's legendary comebacks. "That's bull."

"Kat—"

"This reprimand has nothing to do with the firm's policies and everything to do with control. If you want our friendship to survive another twenty-four years, it's time you wake up and realize I'm not your little sister." She paused. *Take your time. Make the rat squirm before you eat him.*

Kat leaned a little further forward, taking care that her Wonderbra-enhanced chest showed to its best advantage. "You want us to be friends, don't you, Rourke?"

The man she'd seen on more than one occasion slice a multimillionaire into tiny pieces during a divorce case mutely nodded. Lordy, playing with the victim was fun. "I'm woman, all woman." She paused again and watched a bead of perspiration roll down the side of Rourke's face. Time to move in for the kill.

"You have every right to be upset with me." Rourke walked to the front of his desk.

She backed away. Then, again, a small retreat might be in order.

Leaning back against the desk's edge, Rourke slid his thumbs into his pants pockets. Kat swallowed, her gaze drawn to his splayed fingers, then back to his face. She swallowed again as his inspection started at her feet, slowly worked its way up her legs, pausing at her chest before continuing on to her face.

"You're right, I was out of line. Please accept my *sincere* apology."

"You're apologizing?"

"Yes."

"Why?"

"I know Jason and men like him. He has a 'love 'em and leave 'em' attitude."

"On the contrary." Kat strolled over to the sofa, sat down and eased back against its cushions. "He seems to meet most, if not all my criteria."

He folded his arms across his chest. "Is that a fact? How'd you come by this information? Conversation? Or sampling the goods?" Scowling, Rourke stalked to the couch and stared down at her.

"I don't sample goods. I feel them to see if they're good quality." Kat lowered her voice to a purr. "Then, I put them up against me to see if they complement me. You know, feel right against my skin."

"Are you and Jason lovers?"

Lovers? Hell's bells, she'd only been out with the man three times. She'd slept with only one man in all her thirty-one years, Mark. What was going on in that testosterone-driven brain?

More than anything, she wanted to set him straight about who and what she was, but she couldn't. If she did, she'd never be free of Rourke. As it was, she longed for his touch. Heavens, she'd settle for a handshake or a slap on the back. Nope, she had no choice but play the hand she'd dealt herself. "That's none of your business." *The tick in his jaw's back, better be careful, girl.* "But for your peace of mind, no, we aren't lovers. Yet. And just for the record, Jason's different from his reputation."

"Is that a fact?"

"Yes, it is. Jason's always been a perfect gentleman. Which is more than I can say about you."

"A perfect gentleman? Jason?"

Kat flushed. "Yes. A perfect gentleman. With Jason, going to bed with a woman is his secondary, not primary, interest." How dare he arch his eyebrow and give her that condescending smile. "You know, Rourke, it would be nice if you credited me with intelligence in my private life, not just at work. So I've gone through a long dry spell. That doesn't mean I'm planning to jump into the sack with the first man who propositions me. I'm looking for Mr. Right."

"Jason Barrington is *not* your Mr. Right."

"Thank you for determining that for me. Tell you what. I'll run all my candidates by you, and you can rate them for me. That should save us both a lot of time. What do you think?"

"Remember the old saying, there's no such thing as a free lunch. That's true of me and of any man you date. Trust me, Kat, at our age, men will expect more than a good night kiss. A lot more."

"As long as there's chemistry, that's fine with me."

"Ah, yes, chemistry." Rourke smiled and approached. "Tell me Kat, how will you know when the *chemistry* is right?" Squatting before her, he ran a finger softly across her palm and her wrist.

Desire raced through her veins.

Rourke gently cupped her chin. His breath caressed her lips. His mouth brushed hers, then the phone rang.

Kat gulped for a breath. "Saved by the bell," she muttered as he talked to a client. In the last three weeks, she had learned more about chemistry than she'd ever wanted to know. Rising from her chair, Kat inched toward the door.

Rourke dropped the receiver in its cradle and leaned back against the desk. Grinning, he stretched his legs out in front of him and crossed them at the ankles. "Kat, come back here and sit down. We haven't finished our talk."

"You weren't talking."

She hated his indulgent smile. Well, *hate* might be too strong a word, but she sure didn't trust it. Better to stay out of reach. This seemed a definite retreat-bugle moment.

"I'd like to take you out to dinner, tonight. Consider it

lesson number five in our seminar on attraction and eventual seduction. Just name the restaurant," he urged with a rakish grin.

Kat glanced down at her fingernails, then back up at Rourke. "Maybe another time. I already have a date tonight."

His smile disappeared. He pushed away from the desk and moved toward her.

Retreating, she swore on her grandmother's grave she heard a bugle blowing.

"With Jason?" he asked in a low, silky voice, backing her against the door.

"That's right." She licked her lips. "Hmm, I've been thinking."

"Don't." Rourke placed a hand on either side of her head. "Where you're concerned, Kat, I've discovered too much thinking's a dangerous occupation."

She attempted to maintain her composure and ignore his remark. "Asking for your help in learning how to attract men was a mistake. You've slipped back into your big brother mold. I don't need a keeper, Rourke. I'm a grown woman—experienced—and with emotional and sexual needs of my own."

"Are you?" he asked, his voice barely above a whisper.

"Yes! So I want you to forget about my request." She prayed he didn't hear the tremor in her voice. Darn man! Why couldn't Jason, who looked like a perfect Mr. Right make her tremble? "Attracting men isn't hard."

"No doubt you're right." Kat didn't miss the quickly hidden flare of anger in his eyes. "You know, of course, Jason will expect more than a handshake at the door."

"Well, of course he will. This'll make our fourth date."

"Is that a fact? Have you ever experienced the out-of-control sensation of chemistry and what I call lust?" Rourke asked, his breath hot against her ear.

"Yes," she hissed.

"Really? When?"

Kat stared at Rourke's chest. She refused to answer. This was not the way she'd planned her exit. She wouldn't let him get to her. Okay, he'd already gotten to her. But there was no way she'd let him know it.

Forget the plan, go for the kill. Kat lifted her gaze to his. "I hate this one minute hot and the next minute cold business. You said you refused to do anything that endangered our friendship. But you have. One day we kiss and the next you can't get away from me fast enough."

"Now, Kat—"

"Don't you dare patronize me! At the benefit you glared at me all night, then acted the lover on the dance floor. Then, today, you threaten to fire me and in the next minute make a pass." Kat shoved him. "Enough is enough. Let me go."

"No, I don't think so. You're right about my behavior," he said slowly, his fingers tracing the line of her cheek. "It has been inconsistent."

There was no mistaking the raw hunger in his gaze. She tried to duck under his arms. The rat had trapped her, *the Kat*. This was not supposed to happen. She, not he, was the huntress.

Damn, too late, Kat thought as his mouth covered hers. The kiss, which started as surprisingly gentle, soon became urgent and hungry. Kat shuddered as his tongue dueled with hers.

Rourke's breathing came fast and shallow. He reversed their positions, leaned back against the door, and pulled her between his thighs and into the cradle of his hips.

Clinging, moving sinuously against him, passion and desire melded into a single hot, blue-white flame, consuming everything in its path, including her common sense.

Rourke pulled her blouse free from her skirt and slid his hand up under it. He cupped her silk-clad breast, fondling and caressing it. The moment he had the tip of her nipple between his fingers, Kat remembered this was not part of the plan.

Jason, not Rourke, was Mr. Right. Kat placed her palms against his chest and shoved. "Stop. Now!"

Rourke shook his head and took one step back. "Don't say a word," he growled.

"Don't say what? You overstepped the bounds of propriety? Remind you this is an office and Grace's right outside the door? Or quit?" Kat rebuttoned her blouse and jammed it in her skirt. "Which one of the above am I not supposed to say?"

"All of the above," he said in a low, soft voice. "We need to talk, sweetheart."

"Yeah, well, no thanks. I've seen the way you talk." She bent down and retrieved her fallen purse. "Don't 'Sweetheart' me you—oh, you know what you are. And get away from the damn door. Move it, or lose it, Rourke."

He laughed. "Move it, or lose it? What are you planning to do? Knee me? Hit me with that satchel you call a purse? What?"

"Oh, shut up," she muttered. "I want out." *In more ways than one.*

"You're running away, Kat. And that isn't like you. You've always faced life head on. But I understand. You're scared. Scared of your feelings and the passion that explodes every time we touch one another."

Unable to meet his eyes, Kat looked down at her feet. Against her will, she admitted to herself that Rourke's kisses had awakened her passion and left her reeling. And now that he'd pulled back, she felt a sense of disappointment and unfulfillment. It reminded her of a Fourth of July celebration when she was seven. The early fireworks were full of promise, the finale collapsed. A dud. A no-starter.

Kat raised her head. "You're mistaken Mr. Hawthorne."

"Bullshit." Rourke grabbed her arms. "You know better than that and so do I, sweetheart. What happens between us every time we touch is called chemistry. Plain, old-fashioned, uncontrollable desire. Just for the record, it doesn't happen all that often, and when it does, only a fool lets it escape."

Kat realized not only was she out of her league, but worse, desiring him was a complication she didn't need. It was one thing to have an affair with a man. It was quite another to experience real sexual chemistry, explosive chemistry, at that, with her boss, no less. It was a lose/lose situation. Why hadn't she thought of this before following Liz's suggestion? Had she been subconsciously attracted to Rourke all these years?

Maybe. But he still scared her. He could have any woman he wanted, and had. She wanted marriage—not an affair. Yet, Rourke stood there professing what they'd shared was more than lust. It was time she took control of the situation—past time.

Frightened by the knowing gleam in his eyes, Kat lashed out, "Chemistry be damned. It isn't professional for us to be involved. All that'll happen is, I'll lose a friend and a job I need and love."

She grabbed the doorknob, then paused and stared him in the eye. "I was married to a Mr. Wrong. I don't plan to repeat that mistake, no matter what the chemistry. So back off. I'm looking for Mr. Right. And at the moment, Jason's my best prospect."

Kat studied The Prime Rib Bar's understated decor.

Small round tables dotted the room. Alcoves lined walls of dark, walnut paneling. She nudged Jason and whispered, "Doesn't it remind you of the hushed atmosphere of an English men's club?"

"You've been in an English men's club?"

"Every time I read a historical romance."

Jason chuckled. "Ah, Kat, you're good for me. You make me laugh."

Kat returned his smile. She made Mr. Right want to be with her. Now, all she needed to do was generate the chemistry. But how? With Rourke it was there, no need for externals or games. And in this game, she was still in primary school while Jason had finished postdoctoral work.

In the restaurant's mirror, Jason looked every inch the successful Washington power broker.

"Enjoying the view?"

Flushing, she turned and looked up at his laughing ice-blue eyes.

Moments later, the maître d' escorted them to their table. Pride filled Kat at how women of varying ages watched Jason. No doubt, he attracted appreciative glances wherever he went.

"You're very beautiful. I'm the envy of every man here," Jason murmured.

"You're wrong. Every man here wishes he had your success and power and every woman that she were on your arm."

"I wonder," he whispered to her, "are you as guileless as you seem?"

At their table, Jason kissed the tip of his finger and pressed it to her lips. Grinning, he walked to his chair.

"Would you like to order something from the bar before your meal?" the waiter asked Jason once he was seated.

"Nothing for me. Thanks." Jason paused and looked at

Kat. "Would you like another drink?"

"No, thank you. Wine with our meal will be fine." She smiled up at the waiter. "I haven't been here in years. Do you have a recommendation?"

"We are known for our Prime Rib, Crab Imperial, and Red Snapper with a *Vielle Mason* sauce, a rich blend of tomato and basil."

Kat glanced at the menu again. "I'll have the snapper, a baked potato, and asparagus," she told the waiter.

"Prime rib rare, baked potato with sour cream, and broccoli," Jason said absently as he studied the wine list.

With Jason occupied, Kat glanced around the room and caught sight of a familiar raven-haired man. She hesitated, then forced herself to confirm her worst fears. It was Rourke! He wasn't alone. Kat's teeth closed with a snap. Clarissa!

Kat took a deep breath. She was ten kinds of a fool. She squirmed in acute embarrassment as she remembered earlier that day. Rourke had overwhelmed her senses. The heat and passion that had flared between them with the suddenness and violence of an erupting volcano had shaken her to her core.

The entire episode was, without doubt, one of the more humiliating experiences of her life.

Kat frowned. Why was Rourke here, in this restaurant? He hated coming into the city. But then the pond scum also claimed to loathe Clarissa.

Nothing explained his presence in The Prime Rib. He couldn't have gotten a table without a reservation. That meant, he'd planned his date in advance because she sure hadn't told him where Jason was taking her.

Liz!

She watched Rourke and Clarissa talking and laughing. Suddenly, he looked up.

Unwilling to be seen staring at him, Kat turned back to Jason, determined to show Rourke she had Jason's full attention. Unfortunately, at the moment Jason's gaze rested on the wine steward pouring wine into his waiting glass.

Smiling, Jason took the stemmed glass and swirled the deep, ruby-colored liquid, then sniffed the wine. After a sip, he nodded his approval. Once Kat's glass was filled, he raised his glass in a toast. "To us and the future," he said as their glasses touched. "And an exciting journey of exploration together."

CHAPTER EIGHT

Rourke mentally cringed at Clarissa's screech-owl voice. Why hadn't it bothered him during their affair? The reason had nothing to do with her conversational abilities and everything to do with her talent in the bedroom, his burgeoning conscience answered.

Ever since the damn opera, there was no escaping her pursuit. She left messages at the office or on his answering machine at home. And, today, he'd been the perfect mark.

Not five minutes after Kat had stormed out of his office, he'd received a furious call from Liz. On the heels of Liz, Clarissa had called. That's when he'd committed an error a first-year law student wouldn't make. He hadn't listened to Clarissa; he'd obsessed on Jason as Kat's Mr. Right.

Rourke groaned. Damn, Liz! If she hadn't mentioned Kat coming here, he never would have suggested this place. Hell, he hated restaurants that charged a bundle because of location and atmosphere. That he was here was proof an almost forty-year-old man could act as immature as an adolescent.

He exhaled harshly. At least he'd mitigated the damage and suggested they meet here so he wasn't stuck driving her home.

"Rourke, could I have a taste of your dessert? I love their chocolate cheesecake. Its silky texture . . . the way it melts in my mouth."

He looked at Clarissa's crayon-red lips as she ran her tongue across her teeth and grimaced. "If you love it, you should have ordered it."

"But I'm on a diet. Just one little old bite, please."

Rourke scooped the last morsel of his dessert onto his fork and placed it between Clarissa's parted lips. As her lips closed over the dessert, his eyes involuntarily drifted back to Kat. She shot him a killer glare, then turned back to Jason and gave him a bone-melting smile.

After her experiences with Mark, Rourke could just imagine what Kat was thinking. He'd used her in a sadistic game of one-upsmanship. She didn't give her trust easily. Rourke only hoped her faith in *his* integrity wasn't irreparably damaged.

"Rourke! Stop glowering at Jason and Kat and keep your eyes on me. When you suggested dinner, I didn't think you'd spend the evening eyeing every move Kat and Jason make."

He donned his courtroom expression. After an evening in Clarissa's company he understood why a man could become desperate enough to get up, walk out, and never be heard from again.

He gave himself a mental shake. "Sorry. It's been a long day, and tomorrow doesn't look any better. How about calling it an evening?"

"Why not? It isn't as if you're here, anyway."

Rourke motioned to their waiter. "Put it on this," he said, handing the man his credit card.

"Ever since they've arrived," Clarissa waved in the direction of Kat and Jason's table, "you've been watching Kat. No one uses me, Rourke." Clarissa tapped a long, blood-red fingernail against the tabletop. "You'll pay for tonight. I'll make sure of it."

"Be careful what you threaten, Clarissa. You'd hate to see me in court. Especially at the opposing table." Rourke scrawled his name, grabbed his receipt and stalked out, leaving Clarissa to follow him.

* * * * *

Kat smiled at Jason as they strolled up her front walk. Then she stumbled. A terrifying realization washed over her. She had a serious problem. She wanted Rourke, not Jason!

She knew her feelings came from a place deep inside her where common sense didn't exist. No matter how much she wanted Rourke, she couldn't risk an affair, much less marriage. She refused to lose herself again.

He was Number Nine, personified.

She had written that one negative on the list as protection. Kat stumbled again. *Oh, my God!* She'd deluded herself into thinking number nine and five, nixing gray eyes, were the result of her marriage to Mark. But it hadn't been. She'd tried to protect herself from Rourke.

Not that that changed a darn thing. He was still Mr. Wrong and always would be.

Removing the house keys from her purse, Kat felt a tingle of awareness. She glanced behind her and spotted a familiar black BMW parked across the street.

Rourke! Blast and double blast the man. He'd followed her home. Payback time!

A slow and, she hoped, sexy smile played at the corners of her mouth. "Thank you for the lovely evening, Jason. I've really enjoyed myself." Kat tilted her head. "Would you like to come in for a cup of tea or coffee?"

"I thought you'd never ask!" Grinning, Jason took the keys from her hands and opened the door. Then, placing a hand on the small of her back, he escorted Kat inside.

Using the light from the foyer, she walked into the living room and started to turn on all the lamps.

Jason touched her shoulder. "We really don't need all this light, do we?"

Kat jumped. "W-what?" She turned. Triple blast! He'd

followed her around the room turning off or dimming the lamps as he went. Lordy, now what did she do? She'd set the stage and he was only following her directions. Her damned pride was doing it to her, again.

Kat cleared her throat. "No, I don't suppose we do. If you'll excuse me a moment, I'll make myself a cup of tea and you some coffee. Is decaf okay?"

"Coffee?"

"Yes . . . coffee. I did invite you in for some. I thought we could talk and get to know each other a bit better." One look at Jason's baffled expression confirmed her fears. Talking was the last thing on Jason's mind.

"Let's both go to the kitchen? You can keep me company while I get our drinks. I have some homemade fudge brownies. Would you like one topped with ice cream?" When she saw Jason shake his head in frustration, Kat pivoted and walked quickly to the kitchen.

Forty-five minutes later, Kat finally admitted asking Jason inside her home had made her earlier decisions seem brilliant by comparison. The man had a one-track mind. And as much as she liked him and thought he might be Mr. Right, she wasn't ready to move to a higher level of intimacy tonight.

Jason moved his chair closer to hers and covered her hand with his. "Thanks, but I can handle it." Kat gathered their plates and flatware, then hurried to the sink and started putting everything in the dishwasher.

Finished cleaning, Kat picked up her mug of tepid tea and turned back to the room. Jason stood before her, his chest barely inches from her breasts.

I can't deal with this! Kat looked down at her mug of luke-warm tea. With her smile firmly in place, she lifted her eyes up to meet Jason's. She moved her hand, the mug bumped against Jason's chest and upended it down the front of his shirt.

"Oh, no!" Kat's hand flew to her mouth.

"Christ!" Jason took several quick steps backwards.

"Oh, I'm so sorry. So *very* sorry," Kat said, injecting a tremor into it. "I don't know how I could have been so clumsy."

Jason cupped her face. His finger swiped at a single tear. "Don't worry about it, Kat. It's only a shirt."

"But it'll be ruined." She frowned, then smiled. "I know how to get the stain out."

She spun back to the sink, quickly put on her rubber kitchen gloves, grabbed the kettle of hot water, and a clean cloth. "Although it works better if you pour boiling water directly on the stain, I'm sure it'll work if I just dab the shirt with boiling water. It shouldn't hurt much," she said with a gleam in her eyes as she soaked the rag and advanced on him.

"No, no. That's all right. It's a custom-made shirt. The cleaners can take care of it," Jason stuttered, grabbing his tie and suit jacket off the back of a kitchen chair. "I'll phone you," he called from the front room.

"Yeah, sure you will. And pigs fly, too." Kat put the kettle back on the stove. She shook her head. "Stupid move, Kat. Really stupid move." Maybe someday she'd be able to laugh about it, but not now. Not when her best, make that *only*, candidate for Mr. Right had just run out of her house.

Kat switched off the lights then climbed the stairs. As she entered her bedroom, she reviewed Rourke's actions. They represented everything she couldn't abide. Dishonesty. Attempting to control through manipulation. So why did she feel so lost.

Turning, she caught her reflection in her antique cheval

mirror. "Oh, *su-gar!*" She touched the large wet area down the front of her dress. "Nothing's going right tonight."

Reaching behind her, she pulled the zipper down and slipped out of the sodden mess. As she lay the dress on her bed, she discovered her bra, half-slip, and panties were also soaked. Disgusted, she stripped out of her undergarments.

Glancing down at the bed, her eyes rested once again on the stained red dress. She hoped it wasn't permanently damaged. She loved the sheer, fragile material. Its beauty and the way it reflected light reminded her of the gossamer strands of a spider's web.

She slipped into her green silk robe, then gathered up her wet garments and headed back down to the kitchen and the kettle of boiling water.

Kat's front door swung open and Jason strode out. "I ought to kill you," Rourke muttered.

Okay, Kat needed to spread her wings and test her appeal. But this! One look at Jason told Rourke more than talking had taken place. The fact Kat had spotted his car, looked straight at him, then turned a soft, sultry smile on Jason and invited him into her house ate at Rourke like acid.

Hurt, anger, betrayal and frustration blended, fueling each other to create a vicious stew. Rourke got out of his BMW and slammed the door. Striding across the street, he fought to hold emotion in check.

Remember Liz's warning. He would lose her if he displayed the depth and savagery of his feeling.

Kat paused at Tory's room and stared at her daughter's smooth, empty bed. She wished Tory were home, instead of spending the night at Liz's house.

With a sigh, she headed for the stairs and descended.

Kat hesitated on the bottom step as the doorbell rang. Jason? *Maybe pigs do fly.*

Nah! That'd be too easy. There was only one person who'd have the nerve to sit on the bell while banging on her door at twelve-thirty at night.

Squaring her shoulders, Kat marched to the door and put her eye to the peephole. Yup, it was Rourke all right, but not the man she recognized. She had seen him rumpled many times, his tie and jacket off, his hair disheveled, or in his jeans. Tonight was different. In the tight white lines around his mouth, she saw a man struggling to hold onto the remnants of civilized demeanor.

And doing a mighty poor job of it.

Kat closed her eyes and took a deep breath. Why did she suddenly feel weak and vulnerable? Rourke might bluster, but he wouldn't do more than that. She gnawed on her lower lip. Over the last year she'd conquered her paralyzing fear of domineering men. And in the past several weeks, she'd gained a confidence she'd never had. She refused to retreat into the shell she'd inhabited most of her life.

She looked through the peephole, once again, and watched Rourke step back from the door.

"I know you're there, Kat! Open up or I'll open the door myself!"

She knew he wasn't bluffing. Rourke never threatened. He stated what he'd do, then did it.

Kat cinched her robe's belt, then unlocked the door and opened it. "What're you trying to do, wake the dead?" Clutching the neck of her robe closed, she took a step back into the foyer. Their gazes locked, each assessing the other.

Rourke's jaw clenched. His eyes dropped to Kat's silk clad body. Outrage warred with a surge of raw desire as he stared at the swell of her breasts. The outline of her nipples pressing against the thin bathrobe brought a sudden tightening to his groin.

"Shut the door. You're letting all the cool air out and the hot in," she ordered over her shoulder as she stalked toward the kitchen.

Rourke scowled at Kat's disappearing back, then shut and locked the door. Her glare could have melted steel. *Tread gently,* a small voice warned him. "Is Tory asleep?"

"Like you really care."

"Don't give me any grief. Just tell me, did I wake her?"

"If she were here, I'm sure you would have. But since she's at Liz's, it's doubtful. Of course, we could always call and check."

Rourke frowned. "At Liz's!" He'd had enough games for one night. "Guess that's necessary when you don't want your daughter to know you're—"

"I suggest you stop while you still can."

"Do you? Tell me, Kat, was Jason satisfying or are you still hungry and interested in trying me?"

"Jason's all any woman needs. Couldn't you tell by his condition when he left? After all, you *are* parked across the street."

Rourke didn't stop to think. He reached out, grabbed Kat's upper arms, and pulled her to him. His lips covered hers in a kiss filled with hunger and anger.

Shame filled him as Kat struggled free and wiped her mouth with the back of her hand. His gaze dropped to her fingers tightening around the red garment clutched in her right hand.

"Chemistry or no, I need a man who's willing to fulfill the promises his kisses make." She paused and slowly looked him up and down. "Tell me, Rourke, is the problem that you're not man enough to finish what you start?"

Blood pounded in his temples. He pulled himself erect and looked down at her, using his patented courtroom look of contempt. "Oh, I'm man enough to finish. It's just that I don't like leftovers. Even when they're as warm and inviting as you."

Her face paled to chalk white. "You bastard," she hissed. Kat pushed past him and ran up the stairs. Once she reached the safety of the landing, she paused, whirled around and pointed down to the door. "Get out. Get out of my house, Rourke. Now," she whispered in a choked voice.

"Like hell I will!" Rourke yelled after her, taking the stairs two at a time. There was no way he'd leave until they'd resolved this. Because, if he did, she'd never speak to him again. Unfortunately, if he didn't reach her before she shut her bedroom door, she'd lock him out.

Rourke reached Kat's room. Her shoulder was pressed against the door, but she hadn't yet turned the key. Her strength was no match for his. With the palm of his hand, Rourke pushed the door open, sending it crashing against the wall and Kat three feet backwards. Slamming the door shut behind him, Rourke leaned back against it. "I have absolutely no intention of leaving before I get some answers."

From her position on the floor, Kat glared up at him, her features contorted with shock and haughty rebuke. "I didn't realize I was dealing with Conan the Barbarian."

Standing, she straightened her robe and cinched the tie around her. "As with most domineering men, you're nothing but a bully. From this moment on, I'm not talking to you."

Rourke would have pointed out she was incapable of not talking, except Kat's robe had fallen open to the waist and he couldn't keep his eyes off her full breasts.

"I mean it, Rourke. Get out of my house or I'll call 911."

Rourke snorted and folded his arms across his chest.

Kat grabbed the cordless phone from beside her bed. With the phone in her right hand and her stained dress in the other, she advanced. Reaching him, she shook the dress in Rourke's face.

The red gauzy fabric slapped against Rourke's cheek. His gaze narrowed as he recognized the short, backless dress from earlier in the evening and remembered how Jason's hands had touched her exposed skin. It was a matador's cape to his sense of betrayal. He glanced at the unwrinkled bed.

Several conclusions hit him at once. Kat was standing in front of him in a slinky silk thing, instead of the usual ratty pink-terrycloth robe she usually wore.

She also had nothing on beneath the green silk. That was the reason why it had taken her so long to answer the door. She was busy picking her dress and slip up off the floor.

"Were you and Jason in such a hurry you couldn't even make it up to your room?" He reached out and flipped the edge of the dress.

"Yup! I've always wondered what it'd be like standing pressed up against the wall."

"You? Against the wall? I don't think so. You might as well tell me what went on," Rourke said. "I'm not leaving until you do. What happened?"

"Believe what you want. You're going to no matter what I say."

Rourke drew her to him. "With Jason's kisses fresh in your mind, let's see how mine rate."

Stiffening, Kat pulled free of his arms. "I want you to leave, now. I'm sure Clarissa will welcome you."

"Clarissa? Why would I want to go to Clarissa?"

Kat reached up and rubbed her temple. "She was your date. And like you, *I* don't settle for leftovers."

The slamming door shook her fragile composure. Lordy,

why had she ever started this quest? She had lost Rourke's friendship and probably her job. A couple aspirin and a heavy dose of self-pity and maybe she could face getting up in the morning.

Jason cautiously approached Clarissa's table. He didn't like or trust the woman. Worse, under her devouring gaze he felt like a man with his fly open and his family jewels hanging out for the world to see. He adjusted the sleeves of his jacket. This meeting had better be good.

Naturally, Clarissa had tossed him the perfect lure. Kat Snow. She fit his criteria for a perfect wife. True, there were no sparks. But then, who needed them? He was married to his career.

Clarissa had told him she had vital information on Kat—information he had to explore before he proceeded to set the net and snare his prey.

"Dar-lee-ing, I'm thrilled you could make it."

Jason caught himself mid-eye roll. The torture he was willing to go through to get information on Kat, he thought taking a seat. "What's up?"

"I love watching you cross a room!" She leaned forward. "You exude such power."

Coming on a little thick, aren't you, Clarissa? Jason forced a smile. "I doubt anyone but you noticed me." Jason winced at Clarissa's high-pitched laughter.

"Not true, darling. It's a charge knowing everyone in the restaurant realizes we're here together."

"Any man would be honored." He didn't pray often, but he sure hoped to God his manners held out through the entire conversation.

"Of course."

Jason sighed as Clarissa flipped her hair back over her

shoulder and ran her tongue over her bright red lips. Lord help him, the woman was always on stage.

"I guess I should get right to the subject—little Katherine."

"I was curious what you meant by being 'forewarned is forearmed.' " Jason watched in amusement as Clarissa leaned over, allowing him an unobstructed view down the front of her blouse. He had to admit, her last surgeon had done an excellent job on those implants. They'd probably still be perky when her thighs were hanging around her knees.

"Darling, I've known Katherine for years. It's obvious to a woman when another woman, a mere child in Katherine's case, doesn't know her own mind." Clarissa laughed. "Mark's been the only man she's ever known in the biblical sense. I'm sure you've noticed that she's devoted to Rourke. I suppose it was only natural under the circumstances. After all, he's known her since she was a child and then gave her a job after Mark's death. She's such a loyal little thing and afraid of hurting Rourke's feelings. The irony is, he and I want to get married, but gentleman that he is, Rourke wants Katherine settled first."

Jason nodded. "Thanks. You don't have anything to worry about. Kat meets my criteria, and I rarely lose a venture I set out to get." Jason picked up the wine list. "Is there anything else I should know?"

"Well . . ." Clarissa tapped a long fingernail against her lip. "I know most men don't believe in astrology, but I do. And I hope you do too. You see, Katherine is a Taurus. An earth sign."

Jason's mouth dropped open. He started to say something, when she chuckled and placed a well-manicured fingertip against his lips.

"Hear me out. You're about to learn something that even

Katherine doesn't know. Don't let her placid and composed exterior fool you. She's a very passionate woman. I've often wondered why she stayed married to her inept lover of a late husband."

"And?"

"Ah, you see the Taurus woman is a sensual creature. She wants pleasure more than excitement. Touch her frequently, she loves to be fondled and caressed. Once she's in the proper mood, possess her, take Katherine to heights her dullard of a husband didn't know existed."

Jason struggled to keep from flinching as Clarissa traced the crease beside his mouth.

"From personal experience, I know you're more than capable of educating the innocent. And Jason, if you please Katherine, teach her not to fear her body, she has the potential to be as good as me."

"I'm sure she could never come close to being like you." *And that fact alone made Kat desirable!* Clarissa laughed again, and Jason dug his nails into the table.

"Once the little kitten has been smitten with the right Tom-cat, Rourke and I can get on with our relationship."

Jason raised an eyebrow. "I know you said that Rourke and you were an item, but I'm surprised. I thought your break-up a few years back was less than amicable."

"Love, we've always been a couple. We just have our ups and downs. But, then, the bedroom is always the great equalizer, don't you think?" She reached out and drew a blood-red fingernail down his hand. "As I said, we're talking marriage."

A smile curved Jason's lips. "Thanks, in every sense of the word."

"You can count on me to assist you in any way possible. Please, don't hesitate to call—day or night."

Jason ignored the innuendo. "Champagne?" He motioned

to the bottle sitting in an ice bucket next to their table.

"Of course. I think we have every reason to celebrate."

Jason called for the sommelier to uncork the bottle. Once their glasses were filled and they were once again alone, he said, "A toast to our good fortune." *My biggest good fortune will be getting away from this barracuda.*

"To our good fortune." Clarissa lifted her long-stemmed champagne flute and touched its rim to Jason's. "And, to true passion."

Jason had been in business a long time, and as he watched Clarissa he recognized the emotion that played across her heavily painted face. As clichéd as it sounded, it was the thrill of victory.

But for whom?

CHAPTER NINE

Kat dragged herself up to the front porch of Liz's house. Sleep deprivation had become a standard in her life. She didn't know how much longer she could last. It had been going on since the night she'd asked Rourke for help. And after last night's shouting match, she wondered if Monday she'd have a job.

She lifted her hand to knock. The door flew open before the first rap. "Mommy! Look at my new baby-doll. Aunt Liz bought Sam and me one." Tory held up a doll the size of a six-month-old. "Sam and me are havin' a tea party. Wanna come?"

"Not right now, punkin."

"Okay, see ya!" Tory rushed around the side of the house.

Kat walked into the open house and spotted Liz standing in the middle of the living room. "What's the doll all about?"

Liz plopped down on the sofa. "I hope you don't mind. I just needed to hear some laughter."

She sank down beside Liz and frowned. A worried expression marred Liz's usually sunny face. "What's wrong?"

"I'm not sure. Lately, Carl's been working crazy hours. I mean long hours, longer than usual. The night at the opera was the last night we've been together."

Kat patted Liz's hand. "Come on, Liz, Carl's a lawyer. You know how it is with the legal profession. Depending on the case or client, lawyers can work odd hours."

"I called the office last night, and a woman answered. A woman with a very deep voice."

Kat didn't like Liz's defeated tone. "It was probably a secretary."

"No! I know Cara's voice." Liz jumped up from the sofa and began pacing back and forth across the Oriental carpet. "I should, she's been Carl's secretary for ten years. And let me tell you, Cara's voice isn't deep and sexy."

Blast and double blast! Liz was right. Cara's voice was light and high-pitched. "What did Carl say?"

Liz wrinkled her nose. "Are you ready for this? He laughed and then said a client named Todd Smith answered the phone while he was in the bathroom. Yeah, right!" Liz started to cry. "I was so mad I refused to kiss him this morning."

"You can kiss him when he gets home from golf." Kat snickered. "Liz, do you know who Todd Smith is?"

"No. . . ." Liz tilted her head and looked at Kat. "You mean there *is* a Todd Smith?"

"Yup." Kat leaned back against the sofa and grinned. "He and his lover are breaking up and they're drafting a settlement."

"So?"

"Liz, Todd's lover is a man." Kat chuckled as Liz's eyes widened in understanding.

"You mean . . . he's . . ."

Kat looked at her red-faced friend, nodded, then slapped her knee and began laughing.

"Go ahead, make fun of me," Liz said, as she started to laugh herself. "I guess I just had a case of the screaming green meanies—jealousy at its worst." After removing a tissue, Liz handed Kat the box and flopped down beside her. "And I call myself a shrink."

"I wish my problem were that simple."

"What's my brother done now?"

"Last night when Jason and I got home, I spotted Rourke's car parked across the street."

"What?" Liz started to laugh. "Oh, this is rich. Sounds like big brother has a case of the screaming green meanies, himself."

"No. He just has a case of damaged male ego. You know how dictatorial he can be. He ordered me not to go out with Jason and I defied him."

"Mmm-hmm," Liz mumbled. "So what happened after Jason came in?"

"I needed to cool his jets, so I spilled a mug of tea on him."

"You did *what?*" As Kat opened her mouth, Liz waved her quiet. "That's okay, I heard you the first time. Must say, that's an interesting way to cool a hot man down."

"Rourke didn't think so," Kat said.

Liz doubled over, laughing again. "You mean, Rourke had the balls to burst in on you two?"

"Not exactly."

"So, why did Rourke come to your door?"

Kat wrinkled her nose. "I'm not sure. He was ballistic, shouting and banging on my door, before I even opened it. Then he took one look at me holding my tea-soaked dress and undergarments and accused Jason and me of *doing it* on the living room floor."

Liz raised her hand. "Hold on. If you were holding your clothing, what were you wearing?"

"My robe."

"Was it the silk or terry cloth one?"

"The silk one, and before you ask, I was naked underneath. Satisfied?"

"Almost." Liz grinned. "So what'd you say when big brother asked about your doing the dirty deed?"

Kat brushed nonexistent lint off her jeans. "I told him we didn't do it on the floor, but standing, pressed up against the wall." Kat's eyes narrowed as the events of the previous night replayed themselves in her mind. "Okay, so there was some room for misinterpretation, and I shouldn't have lied. But just where does he get the nerve to criticize me when he's bedding Clarissa? You should have seen them together at dinner."

She paused and glared at Liz. "Of course, I wouldn't have had the pleasure of seeing them together if you hadn't told him where I was going. You should have seen him feeding Clarissa his dessert."

"So, did you tell him off?"

"Yes. I told him to go back to Clarissa and I threw him out of the house."

"Bravo!" Liz said, jumping to her feet and clapping. "Well done. Maybe now he'll get his act together and take some action."

"Act together? Take some action?" Kat looked up at Liz. "You're talking in tongues. As for Rourke, he's never going to want to set eyes on me again. And that hurts, Liz. Hurts a lot."

"You're wrong." Liz patted Kat's hand. "But on the off chance you're right, wait here." Liz walked into the kitchen and seconds later returned with a box of chocolates. "Here, have a piece."

"No thanks," Kat said. "I may never eat again."

"Yes you will." Liz sat next to Kat and put her arm around her. "Come on, Kat, have a piece. It's your favorite Belgian chocolate." Liz popped a chocolate in her mouth, closed her eyes and sighed as it slowly melted. "When you get right down to it, the only thing in life you can count on is calories."

Kat carefully placed the box of chocolate on her coffee table. Maybe Liz had the right idea, after all. Chocolate and calories *were* the only two things a woman could count on.

As it now stood, Kat knew she'd feel a whole lot better

once she cozied up to some nice fat grams and gained twenty pounds. Who knew, she and her high-fat Belgian chocolates might actually live happily ever after.

Kat flopped down onto the sofa. Too bad she didn't believe that cock-and-bull rationale. But, what the hey, a woman was only as strong as her needs. And right now, Kat needed the soothing caress from the ambrosia of the Gods.

She removed the box's lid. As she reached in to take one of the "Fruits de Mar," her doorbell rang. She popped the Guylian chocolate in her mouth, got up and headed toward the door.

She sighed as the last of the melted, silken delight slid down her throat, then squinted out the peephole. One peek and her stomach went into revolt. "Damn! Why now?"

Kat cracked open the door. "And what brings you here, Clarissa?"

Clarissa shoved the door, knocking Kat backwards. With a grin, she stepped into the living room, her three-inch spiked heels sinking into the plush carpet. "A spark of kindness. Otherwise, you'd never find me slumming in this neighborhood. I've come to stop you from making a complete fool of yourself."

"I beg your pardon?"

Clarissa rounded the side chair and eased down into it. "That little escapade last night was quite pathetic."

Kat returned Clarissa's smile with a glare. The woman didn't know the meaning of boundaries. But Kat was willing to give Clarissa her due. With a dress cut almost up to the crack all that was missing was a cigarette holder and a Dalmation coat and the woman could have passed for Cruella Deville.

"Escapade?" Kat asked, struggling to keep from snickering.

"Darling, you tried so hard to look at Jason with passionate intent. But you didn't fool anyone. Do you honestly think we missed those childish glances you were sneaking at Rourke? You'll never get him, he's mine. He always has been and always will be. Just concentrate on Jason."

"How kind of you. Be sure to let Rourke in on this development. I'm tired of him showing up on my doorstep after my dates leave." Kat unconsciously reached for the box of chocolates. She popped one in her mouth. "Hmmve un?"

"No thank you, dear. I haven't eaten a bite of chocolate in years, that is unless I'm sharing it with someone."

Kat slowly licked her lips. Her gaze swept Clarissa's reed-thin body. "Guess it's been quite awhile between treats." Kat caught a momentary flash of fury in the other woman's expression before her plastic smile returned.

"As I was saying, Jason's ready to settle down. It's written all over him. Look at how he's continually asking you out. He obviously wants to train a wife from the time she's a puppy. Oops. I mean, kitten, in your case."

Feigning indifference, Kat shrugged. "Cat, kitten, what's the difference? They both have claws."

"Sheath them. I'm not here to fight. Let's just say my intention is to make sure you're happily married to a man who will worship you." Clarissa sighed as she stood up. "I'm afraid I've ruined Rourke for other women. We're like an old married couple. We have our scraps, but eventually we work out our differences."

"In your dreams."

Clarissa chuckled. "Just because he went after you last night doesn't mean he's sexually interested in you. He's only worried about your daughter and the scandal you might inflict on the poor little thing. Rourke knows how incredibly naive you are."

Using every bit of restraint she had, Kat rose slowly, gracefully to her feet. "It's time you leave. Now."

"Darling, I was just going." Clarissa walked to the door, stopped, and looked back. "I know it would kill you to admit it, but I'm only doing this for your own good. Now be a dear, and leave Rourke alone so the two of us can get on with our lives."

"Whatever you say." Kat retrieved the metal tin of Guylian Chocolates and moved forward. "Are you sure you don't want one?" Smiling, Kat held the tin out toward Clarissa. "I mean, you really do look like it's been a long time between bites."

"No!"

Another piece of chocolate disappeared. She held the door open for Clarissa. As the woman started through it, Kat released her hold and it swung forward. "Oh, oh, better be quick. Wouldn't want it to hit you on the way out, now would we?"

Stopping at a red light, Rourke's fingers beat a tattoo on the steering wheel of Clarissa's car. Once again, Kat's parting words repeated like a scratched CD. He glanced at Clarissa and suddenly thought of himself as a plate of day-old beef stew.

Yep, leftovers. He'd had his heart cut out, been seared, covered in the heated juices of anger and left to fall apart. Soon he'd be scraped from the pot and thrown away in the garbage.

"Rourke, why are you staring at me like that? I don't have a smudge anywhere, do I?" Clarissa opened her purse and started to pull out her compact.

"Clarissa, put it away. You look just fine."

"Then why the look of angst, lover? If I didn't know better, I'd think you just lost your best friend."

Rourke shook his head. "Nope." He'd lost more than a best friend. He'd lost the woman he loved. He slanted another glance at Clarissa.

He had to be careful. If she smelled blood, she'd circle for the kill. Enough damage had already been done. And he was responsible for all of it. The moment the light turned green he floored the accelerator.

Moronic, criminally insane were the only adjectives to describe his stupidity in agreeing to this picnic. Unfortunately, stupidity was not a defense in either a court of law or the court of *Kat*.

Never in a million years would Kat buy he was feeling lower than a snake's belly, and when Clarissa showed up on his doorstep he'd agreed—in his weakened mental condition—to a picnic on the Washington Mall.

Nope, if she found this out, his ass was grass and Kat would be the lawnmower.

"Park here. You'll never get a spot up front," Clarissa said with a scratchy whine as she waved at the crowd in front of them.

"Sure thing." Rourke pulled into the last row of spaces, turned off the engine, and watched as Clarissa applied another coat of dark red lipstick to her collagen-inflated lips.

"It wouldn't be little Katherine who's bothering you, would it?"

If he wasn't careful, he'd throw the game. Clarissa could spot a potential foul—not paying sufficient attention to her—faster than an umpire could a line drive going bad.

Time to enter hostile witness mode. Show any emotion around the "screech owl," let her suspect she's hit a nerve, and the bitch would make sure Kat's and his disagreement would become an endless chasm.

"Kat?" He turned in his seat and faced her. "I'm getting

damned sick and tired of hearing Kat's name every time my mind wanders. She's my kid sister's best friend and my firm's CPA."

He lifted Clarissa's fingers to his lips. "Rest assured, my attention is focused entirely on you. When you're with me, no other woman has a chance."

Clarissa giggled. Rourke clutched the armrest of the car, his fingers curling into the butter-soft leather.

"Darling, you're so good for my ego. We need to do this more often. I feel so much younger when I'm with you."

"That's as it should be, my sweet." *After all, I feel so much older*. Rourke opened the door and eased out. "Let's find a nice spot for this picnic of ours."

"How about my bedroom?" Clarissa purred the words.

"Another time. For now, how about a little fresh air and sunshine?"

"But, Rourke, sun is bad for you. All those UV rays. It's better to stay inside, darling."

"Humor me." Rourke pointed toward a tree up the trail. There's a good place to settle down."

"Help me get the basket out of the trunk. I have a treat!" She pursed her lips and threw her long hair over her shoulder. "Beluga caviar, vichyssoise, Norwegian salmon and toast points. All compliments of Frederick of Georgetown."

"Jesus, Clarissa, what's wrong with ham and cheese sandwiches, potato chips and some good conversation?"

"Darling, how middle class! Besides, the caviar was a gift from Jason Barrington. You know him."

"Yes. I do." Rourke's hand clenched around the basket handle as he remembered Jason's long session in Kat's house.

"He gave it to me as a going-away gift. We'd . . . seen each other a few times."

Rourke's hands tightened around the basket. In his

opinion, Jason had overpaid to get rid of the woman. Then again, maybe the gift was symbolic—gut a female fish for her eggs.

"Of course, I'm no longer seeing anyone but you. You always were almost too much for me to handle."

Ice ran down his spine. "We're friends, Clarissa. Nothing more."

"Right, friends." Clarissa drew a fingernail down his sleeve. "Good friends. Now help me unpack."

Rourke watched in disinterest as she lifted foiled cans and containers from the rattan basket. Caviar on a picnic. Amazing how different this picnic was from the one he'd shared with Kat and Tory.

He eased down onto the blanket Clarissa had spread and studied the woman and the repast before him. His gaze narrowed as she withdrew sterling silver cutlery and linen napkins. What he wouldn't give for Kat and one ripe peach!

Rourke glared at a grim-faced Kat and an amused Carl across the conference table. What did she think she was doing? For God's sake, Chambers was the firm's client, not the wife. "Milly's petition is without basis. Bruce's paperwork supports his claim of ownership of the boat." He rustled through the file and withdrew a document. "Aside from the fact the house is in his name only, this proves he purchased it prior to their marriage."

Kat leaned forward. "She's saying he used her money to buy *their* house and defrauded her when he put it in individual ownership. Milly also asserts Bruce gave her the boat as a birthday gift."

"Amazing what good sex can do to a man's brains."

"You should know, Mr. I-Am-The-Expert!" Kat muttered.

116

Rourke inhaled sharply, then slowly exhaled. "This isn't getting us anywhere. You're supposed to fight for our client, not his soon-to-be ex. What's gotten into you?"

"I don't like Bruce's game. He forgot to use a prenuptial to protect his property. So, what's he do? He out and out swindles Milly and now we're finishing the job. And why was he able to do it? Because she stupidly *trusted* him."

"*We are not swindling Milly!* The woman is walking away from Bruce a half a million richer than when she married him two years ago. As for Bruce's actions, trust comes hard when a woman throws herself at every available man."

"Perhaps *Mr. Chambers* was overly jealous and uncertain of his masculinity," Kat threw back.

"Does it really matter?" Carl asked, looking at Kat, a smile beginning to creep onto his face. "We just need to settle this in favor of Bruce Chambers."

"That figures," Kat hissed. "Men always blame it on the woman."

"When the *woman* flaunts her body, wears dresses with slits to her ass and shows skin from every possible angle, what's a man supposed to believe?" Rourke snapped, leveling a hard glare at Kat.

"If you'll excuse me, I'm sure you don't need me for this planning conference." Kat stood and moved to the door. "You have my findings. For what they're worth," she said, softly shutting the door after her.

"It's amazing how concerned you are for truth, justice, and the American way." Carl laughed.

Rourke wanted to disappear. He couldn't believe his and Kat's unprofessional conduct. Thank God only Carl had witnessed their lapse in judgment. "Women. They take everything personally."

Carl nodded. "I love every little whimsical moment of

their unpredictability. That's what makes the sparks fly."

Rourke averted his eyes. "Yeah. Well, those sparks can cause a raging forest fire."

"Why do I have the feeling we're not talking about the Chambers' divorce settlement?" Carl asked.

Rourke glanced in Carl's direction. "How do you tell a woman you're in love with her?"

Carl raised one eyebrow. "Are you talking about saying that to our firm's hard-headed accountant?"

"Don't play dumb, Carl. We both know Liz tells you everything." Rourke shook his head. "Has Liz told you about Kat's list?"

"She didn't have to. They wrote it in our kitchen. You should've heard them." Carl grinned. "Number nine was my idea."

"It just keeps getting better." Rourke propped his elbows on the table and buried his head in his hands.

Carl got up and went over to pat Rourke on the back. "It appears that you, my friend, are destined to a life of working with figures. *All night long*."

On autopilot, Kat picked up the phone's receiver. "Kat Snow. May I help you?"

"I hope so."

"Hi, Jason. I didn't think I'd hear from you after the other night."

Jason chuckled. "I brought it on myself. I want to apologize for coming on too strong."

She eased back in her chair. "It's refreshing to hear a man apologize. Thank you."

There was silence for a moment. "Has someone else upset you?"

His tentative tone disarmed Kat. "Of course not," she

said. "I just . . . that is, of late I haven't really had anyone I could count on."

"You can count on me. If you want to, that is. I'd like to make everything up to you. I have a place on the Eastern Shore where we can relax and get to know each other slowly." Jason hesitated before continuing. "I promise to keep my hands to myself."

Before her common sense could step in and stop her, Kat said, "When do you want to go?"

"How about this Friday? We could spend the weekend, and come back after a leisurely lunch on Sunday."

"I've got to see about a baby-sitter for my daughter. Give me an hour and I'll let you know."

With a clenched fist, Kat jerked her arm down. "Yes!" Mr. Right had come through. She wouldn't tell anyone except her sitter, and Liz, of course. But no way would she let Rourke find out. She didn't need his blustering number nine dictates coming her way.

"Kat? We need to talk," Rourke said, entering her office.

Before Kat could answer, her intercom buzzed and Grace said, "Jason Barrington just called back. He wanted to remind you that the beach gets cold at night so don't forget your jacket."

Shoulders slumped, Rourke turned and left her office.

Kat tried to ignore her feelings of guilt as she packed a few last minute items. It didn't help that Tory watched her every move with an injured air of disapproval. Where did a six-year-old get off making a thirty-one-year-old feel ashamed of going away for the weekend?

"Where are you going, Mommy?" Tory asked for the tenth time.

Kat clenched her teeth, then forced herself to relax. She

refused to be interrogated by her own child. "As I said before, I'm going to the beach with a friend for a few days."

"Is the friend a girl or a boy?" Tory asked, her gaze never leaving Kat's face.

"It's a friend, Tory."

"Is it Uncle Rourke?"

Kat stopped packing, sat down on the bed and put her arm around her daughter's shoulder. "Whatever made you think it was Rourke?"

She hugged her daughter. Her little girl was growing up too fast. "You're right, punkin. My friend is a man. And I really like him." She cupped Tory's face between her hands. "A lot."

"But Rourke loves you and you love him."

Kat stared at Tory in disbelief. "You can just put that idea out of your head, young lady. Rourke and I are friends, old friends, nothing more."

"Uh-huh. You look at him like he's a *big* banana split."

Kat sat momentarily speechless, then laughed. "Rourke's head replacing the cherry on the top of a sundae, I like it." After a few minutes, she sobered. "Rourke's Liz's older brother and an old friend. That's all."

"How come you get all red and can't talk right every time he comes over?"

Kat stood, her hands on her hips, and stared down at her belligerent daughter. "Stow it, Tory. This is a fantasy that'll never come true."

"Grown-ups sure are dumb." Tory shook her head. She picked up her new doll and looked at her. "Did you hear that Eloise? How come grown-ups don't know when they're in love?"

Tory raised the doll to her ear, then looked at her mother as she walked towards the bedroom door. "Eloise says that's so kids can 'splain it to you."

"Thank Eloise for me. Aunt Liz will be here in a few minutes, are you ready?"

"*Mommy,* you packed my stuff first." Shaking her head, Tory slid off the bed and skipped out of the room.

Comfortably seated in Jason's Jaguar, Kat watched the sky changing from gray blue to purple and magenta. "It's hard to believe it's almost Labor Day," she said, looking at the rapidly approaching coast line.

"We'd better enjoy it while we can." Jason deftly handled the sharp turn through the gates of his beach home. "Blink, and in a few months there'll be snow."

"No, tell me it isn't true, not snow." Kat laughed. "And to think I trusted the weather channel and their prediction of this weekend being a scorcher."

"Ah, hot during the day, cool at night."

"In other words, perfect beach weather." Kat glanced at Jason and returned his grin. Okay, so he wasn't Rourke. Who needed the havoc Rourke and his chemistry created? Sure he was sexy and brightened her life. So what? He was also bossy, opinionated, and a general pain in the backside. Whereas Jason's ice-blue eyes twinkled, he had a great body, was mentally flexible, made her laugh, and wasn't a rule-making number nine.

Okay, so he hadn't passed the Tory test—yet. But that was only a matter of time. Once Tory accepted Rourke was mommy's Mr. Wrong, it'd be smooth sailing.

CHAPTER TEN

"You said they'd get married an' we'd be cousins." Sam plopped down beside Tory on her bed.

"It's not my fault. Mommy told your mom that Uncle Rourke's not Mr. Right, but Jason is."

"My mom told Daddy that Aunt Kat's got some kinda fixation," Sam insisted.

"What's that?"

Sam shrugged. "I don't know. Daddy laughed an' said Uncle Rourke has one, too. Then Mommy said no, Uncle Rourke's problem was stupidity an' Aunt Kat wouldn't know her soul mate if they were handcuffed together."

"Soul mate?"

"I don't know what it means. It must be good though, 'cause Daddy pulled Mommy down in his lap an' said he sure liked her being his soul mate an' then they got mushy and started whispering."

"I gotta get my Mom home." Tory drew her knees to her chest.

"Pretend you're sick."

"I'm not good at pretendin'." Tory scrubbed at her teary eyes.

Sam bounced on the bed. "You can take the medicine Mom gave Joey after he ate all her birth pills."

"Birth pills?"

"Yeah. The little pink ones in the funny case." Sam wrinkled her nose. "It made Joey throw up."

"Will I get kinda sick or real sick, throw up my guts sick?"

"Joey only threw up two times."

Tory frowned and shook her head. "I gotta get sicker than that."

"So take lots." Smiling, Sam jumped off the bed and ran out of the room.

While Sam was gone, Tory gave Eloise another bottle and thought about her mother rushing back to take care of her. Uncle Rourke had to be there too. He was going to be her daddy. She just knew it.

"Here it is," Sam whispered, handing Tory the bottle. "It's almost full. Remember, take lots."

Tory grinned, brought the bottle to her lips and downed the contents.

With Jason at her side, Kat walked along the shore. "What a beautiful spot." She looked at the solitary point and the sand bar running next to it. "This place is heaven."

"Glad you like it. The place has been in the family for years." He chuckled, kicking up wet sand with his bare feet. "I always feel like a kid when I'm here."

Kat stared at Jason. Love and chemistry were overrated commodities. Honesty, fidelity, and perseverance, those were qualities that stood the test of time.

She ran out into the water and stood knee-deep with waves lapping at the hem of her shorts. "Come on in. It's great."

"Be careful! Sharks sometimes come in close to shore."

"No sharks here," she said with a laugh, after a glance around. "Jason. Jason. Jason. Don't tell me you've let *Jaws* scare you out of wading at the beach." Kat lifted her index finger and gestured him toward her. Boy, playing the vamp was fun. Just think of all the enjoyment she'd missed. As he narrowed the distance, she opened her arms. "Come to me and let me reward you for your bravery."

Jason laughed. "You're a tease. And all teases must pay."

"Oooh, I'm *sooo* scared." Laughing, Kat turned and raced through the surf. "Catch me if you can!" she shouted over her shoulder.

"Jesus-H-!"

Kat stared in horror as Jason's expression became pain-filled anguish. He moved forward a step, then fell to his knees in calf-high water.

She thought she heard him say "Damn!" but couldn't be sure. A wave curled over his head.

Kat started toward him. As she neared him, he yelled, "Stay where you are. I just stepped on a Portuguese man-of-war."

Ignoring his order, Kat raced to Jason's side. "You need help." She knelt and had him wrap his arm around her shoulders. Together, they struggled to their feet and hobbled from the water.

"Are you sure it was a man-of-war and not a regular jelly-fish?"

Jason collapsed on the hard-packed sand and examined his left foot. "I'm sure. There's no missing that purple tentacle. After the fact, of course."

Kat winced. "Of course." She knew all about the Portuguese man-of-war. As a teen, she, Liz and Rourke had spent a week at the beach. On the second day, she'd gotten badly stung by one of those purple-tentacle monsters.

Her foot had looked like someone had sliced it, then it'd swollen to balloon proportions. Poor Rourke, he'd been stuck entertaining her for the rest of their vacation.

Kat bit her lower lip. "Do you want me to call a doctor?"

"No. Just help me to the house. I want to get out of these wet things." Jason rubbed his instep. "It isn't that bad. And I refuse to let that fish ruin our weekend."

Despondent, she sat down beside him. "I'm so sorry. If I hadn't insisted you join me this would never have happened."

Jason traced her cheekbone with the back of his knuckle. "No mortal man could have resisted your invitation."

Kat leaned over and pressed a kiss to his lips. Jason drew her closer and deepened the kiss. Drat, where were the fireworks? She'd felt them all with Rourke. Star bursts. Cloud-bombers. And Big-reds. So why were sparklers all she felt with Jason, her Mr. Right?

Carefully, she eased out of Jason's embrace.

"Ah, Kat. We're going to have a great time."

"I hope so." The fire in Jason's eyes told her she might have missed the Fourth of July explosions but he hadn't.

"Let's go." Jason struggled to his feet. "A small accident like this will not spoil our good time. Once I've changed, let's take the boat out. I can sit and drive at the same time. You don't need sea legs to navigate," he tapped his head with his index finger and winked, "just sea brains."

As Liz returned to Tory's hospital room, Rourke looked up. "Did you reach Kat? Is she coming home?"

"I don't know." Liz shrugged. "Jason's place doesn't have an answering machine so I had to leave a message with the police."

"And?"

"I asked them to track them down and tell Kat Tory's at Fairfax Hospital."

"Are you sure you got the right number?"

"Yes. Jason's aide gave me the right number." Liz glanced down at Tory. "Let's take this out into the hall."

Moments later, Rourke stared down at Liz. "If Barrington has anything to do with it, Kat will never get your message."

"You don't think Jason would keep this kind of information from her, do you? He knows how important Tory is to Kat."

"Liz, don't be so naive," Rourke said. "Jason isn't interested in a long relationship with Kat. All he wants is a conquest. It only takes one night for that."

"Especially when you, my dear brother, played right into his hands and sent Kat running into his arms."

Rourke clenched his hands into tight fists. "What do you mean by that remark?" he said in a low, controlled voice. "And, don't try to B.S. me with your psycho-babble."

"I meant just what I said. If you'd admitted your own feelings about Kat, this would never have happened. But no, you had to be macho-man, ordering Kat about, telling her who she could see and where she could go. Jeez, you'd think you'd have learned your lesson with Mark."

A Maryland State Police car stopped in front of Jason's house. The trooper eased out from behind the steering wheel, adjusted his hat and hitched his gun before moving toward the door.

He rang the doorbell several times. When no one responded, he took out a pad, wrote a note and stuck it in the crack between the front door and doorjamb.

With military precision, he returned to his cruiser and drove off.

"You were supposed to hold the line. What happened?"

"I slipped on the deck and dropped it."

"No kidding." A wave pushed Jason further from the boat. "The current's against me. Throw the ring before I'm out to sea."

"Here it comes!" Kat tossed the white ring and prayed it landed in the water and not on Jason's head. When it splashed just in front of him, she exhaled a sigh of relief. Once he'd hooked his arm around it, she pulled him to the boat.

Jason hadn't cursed or called her names once. At the rate things were going, he'd be canonized for sainthood. Hells bells, she'd nominate him herself. "Just hang on, I'll tow you to the stairs."

Moments later, Jason grasped the ladder, and Kat tied off the ring. At Jason's growled, "Why doesn't this damned thing have an elevator?" Kat leaned over the side of the boat and stuck out her hand. "Grab on and I'll help you up."

"No thanks. With our luck, you'd end up in the drink, too." He shot her a weak smile. "Don't worry, I can manage. Just give me time. With only one good foot, it'll take a bit longer."

She winced. The foot injury wasn't her fault, but this one she owned. He'd given her only one job, anchor the line while he checked the crab pots they'd dropped an hour earlier. But she'd make it up to him. Prove that she was worth the trouble.

Teeth chattering, Jason collapsed on the deck of the sail boat.

Kat wrapped an army-surplus blanket around him she'd found in the storage bin. "You're too wet and cold to sail home. Even with this blanket, the potential for hypothermia's a real problem."

"Gee, and here I'd hoped for a burial at sea."

"Funny man." Kat continued to rub Jason's arms with brisk movements born of terror. "You should get out of those wet clothes."

"I'll be fine. They'll dry soon enough." Jason scooted over to the tiller. "It's low tide, so we're only three minutes from shore." He winked. "How about we build ourselves a bonfire? You like bonfires, don't you?"

Hope blossomed. There was still a chance. Besides, by the

end of the weekend, she might be hearing a choir of angels singing every time Jason looked at her. "I love bonfires."

Kat glanced at Jason. "You're looking better. You've lost that lovely shade of blue."

"I'm almost there."

"I'll add some more driftwood. You'll get warm faster."

"Good idea." He flashed her a grin, then turned his gaze back to the blaze and plopped down on the sand a couple feet from the fire.

She scurried around, gathering what wood she could find. The man had been a real champ about all the mishaps he'd endured at her hands. There didn't seem to be a mean bone in his body. But looks were deceptive. *The Wall Street Journal* called him *The Shark*.

That good old boy charm of his was critical to his success; it lulled opponents into not seeing him coming in for the kill. She'd seen it at work. Not his, but Rourke's. Rourke handled opposing counsel the same way. He especially loved playing the backwoods, country boy with Eastern or West Coast attorneys. Amazing how stereotypes could work in someone's favor and not against them.

What if Jason were a Number Nine but had learned to hide it? She frowned. Naw, that was impossible. Number nines always revealed themselves. All it took was someone thwarting their plans, and she'd done that in spades today.

Kat marched back to the bonfire and smiled down at Jason. She wished he didn't watch her every move, but given his experiences today even the most trusting soul would be wary around Kat the Jinx.

With a swallow, she tossed the wood on the blaze. Flames leapt up and out. Jason closed his eyes, hunched his back to the fire and sighed. "Ah, that's great. Thanks."

"Don't mention it." Kat frowned. He was too close to the fire. No, make that his poncho-like blanket was too close to the fire. Gnawing on her lower lip, Kat mulled over her options. If she told him to move forward a little, she'd sound like his mother. Not the thing if you wanted to be seen as Ms. Right.

Kat ambled back to her blanket and collapsed on the olive-green wool. Leaning back on her elbows, she closed her eyes. By the end of the weekend, she'd prove Jason was Mr. Right and Rourke Mr. Wrong.

There was chemistry somewhere between them. There had to be. Rourke couldn't be the only man who made her bones sing.

"Kat?"

"Hmm?"

Jason sniffed the air. "Do you smell something burning?"

"Burning?" Her eyelids drifted open. Flames licked up the back of his wool, cape-like blanket. "F-fire!"

"Not the bonfire, something else."

Jason sniffed again. "Hair," he said at the same moment Kat yelled, "You!"

The emergency room doctor motioned Rourke and Liz back inside the cubicle.

Rourke rushed to Tory's bedside. He swallowed at the sight of a pale miniature Kat with an IV in her arm. "Is Tory going to be all right?" he asked in a soft whisper.

"She'll be fine," the gray-headed physician said. "A full bottle of Ipecac led to the vomiting and dehydration. But don't worry, she'll bounce back. Six-year-olds are resilient. If she continues responding, we'll release her in the morning."

At Rourke's nod of assent, he said, "I'm glad you're here Mr. Snow; we need to talk." When Rourke opened his mouth to speak, the doctor continued. "This was a cry for attention. Tory was lucky this time. She used Ipecac. Next time—" He shrugged.

"My name's Hawthorne, not Snow." Rourke glanced at the doctor's identification card and added, "Doctor Pace."

Doctor Pace frowned. "I'm sorry. I just assumed you were the father. Judging from the way Tory clung to you, she loves you."

Before he could answer, Liz stepped forward. "Rourke is my brother, Dr. Pace, and Kat, Tory's mother, is my best friend."

"I see." Doctor Pace stared at Rourke. "Let's move out into the hall." Once he closed the door to Tory's room, he turned his attention to Rourke. "Where's the child's father?"

"He died two years ago."

"Then who signed the consent forms?" Doctor Pace demanded.

"I did," Rourke said. "Don't worry, I'm an attorney. All the *i*'s were dotted and the *t*'s crossed." Rourke scowled at Dr. Pace's open skepticism. "When Kat and Tory moved back here from New York, she signed up for your pediatric emergency admission program."

"Good. Back to the death of Tory's father. Could his death be what triggered this incident?"

"No!" Liz said. "My daughter, Sam, confessed everything. According to Sam, Tory wanted her mother home and not at the beach with a friend for the weekend. She wants her mother and Rourke, here, to be together. To that end, she drank a full bottle of Ipecac."

"Given her open affection for you, Mr. Rourke, I'd say my patient is determined you'll be her father." Doctor Pace pulled a pen from his jacket pocket and began writing in Tory's chart.

Rourke closed his eyes. He loved Tory as if she were his own. He also loved her mother and wanted both of them in his life. Permanently.

Rourke's eyes flew open. He had done it again! He was so afraid of losing her, he had driven Kat into the arms of another man. With his luck, she'd probably come back with an engagement ring on her finger like the last time.

Doctor Pace snapped the chart closed and looked at Rourke. "Mr. Hawthorne, if it's possible, could Mrs. Snow return this evening? Tory's been calling for her."

Rourke look again at the little girl lying in the bed. Even asleep, she looked lost and frightened. His jaw tightened. "I'll see to it, myself." Rourke turned to Liz. "Do you have Jason's address?"

"Yes. His aide gave it to me in case we needed it," she said, pulling a piece of paper from her pocket. "Here."

Liz watched Rourke grab his jacket from the corner chair, and strode out the automatic doors. As the doors slid shut behind her brother, she turned back to Doctor Pace. "Thanks, Tom. I owe you. You played your part beautifully."

"I hope you know what you're doing, Liz. The man looks ready to commit murder."

Kat glanced at her watch, then returned to her vigil beside the closed bathroom door, willing it to open. How long did it take to shower and get rid of sand in your hair? Twenty minutes should have been enough. But an hour and a half? Not that she blamed Jason for hiding behind a locked door. Being around her was turning out to be more dangerous than drinking from Typhoid Mary's cup.

Why were the gods punishing her like this? She prayed for her Mr. Right, and they'd sent him to her. Her eyes narrowed in a deep frown as the truth slammed her with the force of a tidal wave.

She was jinxing herself. Jason might be Mr. Right, just not hers. It seemed Mr. Wrong was her Mr. Right.

A click reverberated in the quiet hall. The door opened and Jason emerged wearing khaki shorts and a polo shirt. "I never thought I'd get rid of the sand." He rubbed his head, leaving clipped tufts of hair sticking up. "Guess I'm not the barber I thought I was."

Kat fled the hall and ran into the dining room. *Please, God, in your mercy and benevolence, don't let me laugh.* Sucking her lower lip between her teeth, she watched him hobble toward her with his swollen foot as tremors of silent, hysterical laughter racked her body.

"Don't cry, Kat. I'm okay."

Kat grabbed a napkin off the table and mopped her face dry. "Did you get all the singed parts?" she croaked.

"I think so."

"Would you like me to check? Maybe I can even it a little," she said with a quiver in her voice.

"No offense, Kat. But scissors are the last thing I want in your hands around me."

"But—"

"Don't worry about it. I'll call Male Cuts tomorrow. Given my schedule, Janey's used to making house calls." He flashed her a lopsided grin. "Cheer up. She's a genius. She'll repair the damage."

Kat cleared her voice. "Umm, the only repair will be a GI cut. You know, a buzz cut?"

Shoulders slumped, Jason covered his face with his hands and moaned, "Oh, God! I've become one of the few good men!"

132

CHAPTER ELEVEN

The wail of a siren filled the night. Rourke glanced at the speed-ometer. He'd been clocked at ninety. "Damn! That's reckless driving."

It was his fault. He knew better. At five miles over the limit, a Beemer proved an irresistible target for the-end-of-the month ticket quota. At twenty-five over the limit, it turned into a bright beacon screaming come and get me.

"Good going. You just had to break the law on the DelMar Peninsula, didn't you?" He'd be sleeping on a cot in a six by nine cell while Kat would be laying naked on silk sheets with Jason Barrington.

Rourke eased off the gas pedal and slowly came to a stop. He refused to give the cop satisfaction and hit the brakes. Turning off the ignition, he glanced in his rearview mirror and winced as the officer straightened his hat, hitched his gun and ambled up to the BMW.

"Great! Dudley Doright of the Highway Patrol." Rourke lowered his window and got his wallet.

"Your license and registration, please?"

Rourke handed the man the requested items through the open window.

The officer shone his light first on Rourke's license, then his face. "Are ya aware, suh, that ya were goin' twenty-five miles over the limit?"

"No, sir. I'm afraid I was focused on only one thing. My goddaughter. She's been admitted to Fairfax hospital—"

"Fairfax is the other way, suh!" The cop whipped out his

book and flipped to an empty page.

Rourke could have lived the rest of his life without hearing the heavy sarcasm in Dudley Doright's heavy drawl. "When we couldn't contact her mother by phone, we notified the state police and I took off to get her."

"Where's the mama?" The officer pulled a pen free from the ticket pad.

"Jason Barrington's beach house," Rourke said, forcing a smile as he said the man's name.

"Jason Barrington of Barrington Industries?"

"Yes."

"I took a message there myself. Left it on the front door." The officer replaced his pen, closed his pad and handed back Rourke's papers. "Mr. Barrington lives just off the next exit. Down one mile, then turn right. Ya be more careful with your speed next time, Mr. Hawthorne. Ya hear? I'd hate to see ya end up a statistic."

"Yes, sir."

Rourke watched the officer return to his car and drive off. Perverse it might be, but he'd rather have spent the night in jail than be free because of Jason Barrington's name. Rourke shook his head. No, he wouldn't. That would mean Tory would be without her mother and Kat would spend the night in Jason's arms.

Jason checked the charcoal's temperature. "How do you like your steak?"

"Rare. Texas rare."

"Got it. In the meantime, let's enjoy the steamed crabs. All they need is one quick turn in the microwave." Jason took the plate, piled high with the burnt orange shells over to the microwave and set them inside.

"What can I do to help?"

"You're here to unwind, remember?"

"At least let me make the salad."

"No need. Our housekeeper fixed everything, including the table, before she left for the night. Face it, it doesn't require a great deal of talent to nuke a couple of potatoes and grill steaks."

It killed her seeing Jason hobble around carrying platters of food. Kat moved up beside him. "I can nuke the crabs."

Jason jumped, almost dropping the platter of crabs, then laughed. "I can handle it. I think you'll like them. I defy you to tell the difference between fresh steamed and re-heated via a fast nuke."

The microwave's buzzer overrode Kat's rebuttal.

Jason removed the crabs and set them on the kitchen table. "Let's dig in."

Kat sat down at the table and stared at the mound of hot crab, covered in Cajun spices. "I love crab." Her fingers prodded the pile. "But I've always bought it shelled."

Jason looked up. "Then it's time someone taught you. And you're in luck; you're with the expert."

Kat sighed. Another expert. What was it about men that they were *all* experts?

Jason flipped his crab onto its back and pointed at the belly. "See this long thing coming down?"

"The thing that looks like a soda can's tab?"

"Right, but it's called the apron. Just copy what I do."

Rourke pulled into the driveway and parked beside Jason's Jag. He glanced at the front door and spotted the note. Obviously, they hadn't left the house. They were probably in the back or on the beach.

At least, he hoped so. He wouldn't be able to handle finding Kat in *The Shark*'s bed.

Easing out of his car, Rourke headed around the side of the house. As he entered the rear gardens, he spotted the kitchen lights on and headed for the stone patio, then stopped.

"Pull it and you'll get the treat of a lifetime."

"Slippery little devil, isn't it?"

Slippery little devil? He was too late!

Kat jerked the tab. The shell separated from the crab and sailed through the air like Tory's Frisbee.

Jason's hand flew to his cheek.

"I'm sorry." Kat battled tears as blood seeped out from under Jason's fingers. "I just can't do anything right." It was a good thing Jason wasn't her Mr. Right. She doubted he'd survive marriage to her, assuming he lived out the weekend. Guilt-ridden, Kat stood and moved cautiously toward him.

Jason bolted to his feet. "Stay where you are." He edged around her and started toward the bathroom.

Kat advanced. "I know what to do. After all, I am a mother of a six-year-old."

"She's lived that long?"

Tears streamed down her cheeks. "I'm so sorry." Her fingers touched Jason's newest wound. A noise caught her attention. She turned and glanced at the open French doors. Rourke stood in the threshold looking like a savage warrior bent on murder.

Her hand dropped to her side, and she offered a tentative smile as he advanced toward them. "Rourke? What are you doing here?"

"Thank God! I'm saved!" Jason said, seconds before Rourke's fist connected with his jaw.

"Get your stuff. Tory's in the hospital."

Kat stared at Rourke's disappearing back. "Wait!" she

screamed. "What do you mean Tory's in the hospital?"

Four minutes later after some hurried explanations, Kat stood beside the open passenger door and watched Rourke toss her bags into the trunk and slam the lid down. "You don't understand."

"I said, get in the car, Katherine."

Kat slipped into the car and jerked the door to her. This was ridiculous. She hadn't done anything to deserve this frigid treatment, and Tory wasn't in danger. Of course, Rourke did see everything in black and white.

"Thank you for coming out here. I'll feel better once I see Tory's okay for myself." At Rourke's glower, Kat winced.

"That's nice. God knows we all want you to feel better."

A sharp retort threatened, but Kat bit her lip and watched in silence as Rourke threw the car in reverse. "I realize she's dehydrated, but it was Ipecac, not poison."

"Which she drank because she wanted you home, not off for a weekend of love with your flavor of the month. Or is it, the week."

"That's unfair and out of line. Yes, Tory didn't want me to date Jason. But that's because she wanted *us* together." Kat glanced at Rourke's grim mask and sighed. "Of course, kids dream the silliest things."

Rourke jerked the steering wheel to the right and pulled to the side of the road. "You discussed Jason and this trip with her?"

When Rourke turned a slate-gray glare on her, Kat nodded. "I tried to explain—"

"I don't want to hear it." Rourke faced front, put the car in gear and went from zero to seventy in less than six seconds. "That's always been your problem, Katherine, you don't think."

Kat wasn't sure which was worse, his burning glare of disgust or the cold frost of disdain. She'd never liked her name, Katherine, and now she hated it.

"You couldn't even wait to make it out of the living room to start jumping the man." He snorted and shook his head. "I'm glad you didn't take me up on my offer. I'm not into S&M or having my bed partner draw blood."

"Now wait a minute! That isn't what happened. Jason was showing—"

"His equipment."

Kat gasped. What an arrogant bully! Boy, was he going to be embarrassed when he discovered the truth. "No. I was learning how to pull—"

"A zipper. I can't believe you called his equipment a 'slippery little thing.' I thought I taught you not to attack a man's ego."

"Rourke, if you'd just lis—"

"I shouldn't have slugged him. 'Specially given your put down." Rourke exited the freeway and pulled into a twenty-four hour gas station. He slanted her a look of disgust. "Hell, I'd probably have thanked someone for rescuing me, too."

"Rourke, if you'd just let me—"

"We're almost on empty. Excuse me." He opened the door and eased out from behind the steering wheel.

Fuming, Kat ignored Rourke as he shoved his credit card in the gas pump's card reader, then started to fill the car. The blasted man was impossible. He was worse than a Number Nine. He'd jumped to the wrong conclusion and now refused to hear any evidence that might change his self-righteous verdict. Oh, no, he was Mr. Perfect. He *never* made mistakes.

One look at the eerily composed face confirmed she could forget filing an appeal tonight. She watched him ease behind the steering wheel.

"I love Tory, love her as if she were my own. But under the

circumstances, it would be better if we didn't see one another outside of the office."

Kat swallowed. Sure, they shared chemistry, and it was explosive. So was nitroglycerin. That's why both he and the nitro wore *Handle With Care* tags. One wrong move and you were dead. And her going to the beach with Jason had been an error of explosive proportions.

Well, he could go to hell for all she cared. No way would she ever enlighten him. Let the jerk think what he wanted. The Neanderthal wasn't worth another minute of her time. She refused to spend another second thinking about him.

If he wanted her out of his life, then so be it.

"If that's what you want, fine."

Rourke threw his arm over his eyes. If he could just erase the memory of Kat trying to plead her case. Damn it, he'd blown it big time. Five minutes after cutting her off, it had dawned on him nothing had happened.

Correction, a lot had happened, and all of it to Jason. The poor bastard looked like he'd gone through a war.

Rourke knew *The Shark* would extract his revenge. He fully expected the police to arrive, arrest him for assault and take him off in cuffs. Hell, it was perfect justice. He could just see *The Washington Post*'s business page headline. "Injured Industrialist Sues Prominent Local Attorney for Assault."

Yeah, that would be classic Jason. Silently circle, then move in for the kill. Rourke groaned as his side gate slammed shut. Here it comes, the police.

He eased out of the patio lounge chair and braced himself. He'd take it like a man and plead temporary insanity. Yeah, that should work. Blind, unreasoning jealousy had to be a form of madness. And if it wasn't now, it would be after he'd won and made case law.

"What the . . . What're you doing here?"

"I'm here to see you, darlin'," Clarissa answered in a low purr. "Don't worry about your reputation. It's safe. I parked my Porsche around the corner."

Rourke clenched his teeth. He wasn't in the mood to deal with this viper. All he wanted was complete silence and peace—no laughter, games, or fun. He accepted being alone in his misery and awaiting his punishment, but he drew the line at cruel and unusual. And the smiling woman before him qualified on both counts.

"What do you want?" His eyes narrowed at her batting eyelashes and model slouch stance.

"Why, Rourke, I've come to save you."

"Save me?"

"Of course." Clarissa trailed a long fingernail down his bare arm. "From yourself."

Rourke stepped back from Clarissa's touch, then mentally cursed himself as she followed him. "I wasn't aware I was in need of saving."

"Oh, but you are." Clarissa kept touching Rourke and advancing on him as he retreated from her caresses. "I heard about last weekend. Such a shame about Tory and Kat. But," she gave a small shrug, "not surprising. I also hear you've immersed yourself in work and are endangering your health. All work and no play makes Rourke a dull boy, indeed . . . especially over Labor Day weekend."

Rourke grimaced when Clarissa ran her nails through his chest hair. He peeled her off him and tossed her aside. He couldn't believe it. The woman was wired into the happenings of his life better than the *Washington Post* was to Capitol Hill.

Once again, he shook his head and gathered his wits. "Have no fear, Clarissa, I'm not in danger of keeling over. I don't mean to be rude, but I was just going to—"

"Swim," she said, finishing his sentence. "Yes, I gathered as much. After all, you are standing beside your pool wearing nothing but a tight-fitting Speedo." She smiled up at him as her hands moved to the tie of her sarong-style skirt. "It must be karma. I'm wearing my swimsuit, too."

Rourke's hands knotted into fists at his side. "So I see." He knew his derision-laden words had washed off her well-oiled body as surely as water from his pool would. Clarissa had planned this *impromptu* get-together with great care. Getting rid of her wouldn't be easy. Better to invite her in, let her think she'd won, and then toss her out when his niece and nephew arrived.

"I'm expecting company. And you aren't part of the party," Rourke said, diving into the cool, inviting waters of his kidney-shaped pool and started swimming laps.

After fifteen minutes of vigorous exercise, he stopped at the shallow end, only to discover Clarissa beside him.

Was there no escaping this woman?

When she reached out to touch him, he placed her hand on the pool's edge and swam into deeper water. "Okay, Clarissa, what's with the seduction routine?"

"Grouchy aren't we?"

Rourke didn't miss the flare of her nostrils or the glint in her eyes. He'd seen them before. It was a declaration of war. One she didn't plan to lose and if she did, it would cost the victor plenty.

Rourke shoved a hand through his hair. She promised to make him pay for ignoring her at dinner. With his luck, she'd have him arrested for attempted rape. He had to get her out of here and fast.

"I knew you'd realize I was the woman for you once little Kat was knocked off her pedestal."

Disgusted, Rourke moved a step closer toward the pool's shallow end. "What are you talking about?"

"It's the talk of the town. Jason and Kat at his beach house. You showing up because the twerp daughter got sick." Clarissa moved to him and framed his face between her hands. "I'll admit I've never liked her hold over you, but I didn't want you hurt."

Forcing down his urge to strangle the woman, Rourke jerked free. "Of course you didn't. Otherwise, how could you have *your* revenge."

"Too true." Clarissa's head fell back as laughter erupted from deep within her. "Oh, God, I'd have given anything to have seen when you caught innocent Katherine in *flagrante delicto*. It's just too, too rich."

Rourke grabbed her shoulders and shook. "Nothing happened." Except he'd almost killed the poor sap and now faced potential disbarment.

"Then why's Jason walking around with a bruised jaw?"

Revolted with himself and the woman clinging to him, he grabbed Clarissa and threw her into the pool's deep end. He quickly covered the distance to the nearest edge and hoisted himself up onto the tiles.

"I need a shower." He glared down at Clarissa. "Even chlorine can't wash the stench of you off. When I get out, you'd better be gone."

CHAPTER TWELVE

Kat stared at Rourke's closed front door. She wiped her damp hands on her shorts and took several deep breaths. She pressed the doorbell, surprised the sound could be heard over the beating of her heart. As the handle turned, Kat braced herself for Rourke's hostile reception.

Kat struggled to breathe. The hope she'd held in her heart shriveled and died. "Clarissa."

"My, my, you have impeccable timing. But, then, you always have."

"Don't I though." Kat forced all emotion from her face. She hadn't fallen apart when she'd walked in on Mark and Clarissa in *her* bed and she wouldn't, now. "I'm not here to talk about your dirty past." Kat moved to brush past her nemesis.

Clarissa's eyes narrowed to slits, and she barred the entrance. "I didn't invite you in. In fact, according to Rourke," she paused and licked her lips as a slow smile started, "the two of you are getting ready to go your separate ways, not just as friends but at the office, also."

As Kat felt the blood drain from her face, she took an involuntary step backwards. "Where's Rourke?" She wanted to scream when she heard the hoarse whisper that passed for her voice.

"In the shower. Between swimming and," Clarissa gave a small shrug, "other things, he needed one."

Kat swallowed back the rising bile. How could Liz have been so wrong? Rourke didn't love her. He might have been briefly attracted to the new and different Kat, but not enough to stay away from this witch.

She should have known better. The signs were there for a blind man to read. He and Clarissa were an item. She'd known that even when Rourke had kissed her silly in his office. As she started to turn away, Kat stopped.

Something was wrong. The numbers just didn't add up. Liz hated Clarissa. She didn't allow her children near the woman, and Rourke knew that. He'd never have Clarissa here when he was expecting Sam and Joey. Frowning, Kat studied the smug woman. "I don't believe you. I want to see Rourke, now."

"Sorry, he really is in the shower. You can hang around and talk to him when he gets out. Personally, I have more pride than that."

"Pride?" Kat snorted. Where Rourke was concerned, she no longer had any. Her stiff-necked pride was what had created most of her problems. That and thinking if she loved another powerful, arrogant, and domineering man she'd once again lose her sense of self.

Rourke wasn't Mark. Sure, he was a number nine, but he didn't consider woman objects, possessions.

"Well, are you coming in?"

Clarissa's question snapped Kat to attention. "Of course."

"Suit yourself. I'll only be a few minutes." Clarissa picked up her purse. "I promised Rourke I'd buy some ice cream. Aside from good eating, it has so many other uses."

Kat froze and Clarissa grinned when Rourke yelled from the master bedroom, "Are you still here, Clarissa?"

"I was just leaving, darling," she called back as she walked out the front door.

Rourke's question and Clarissa's answer battered Kat's

senses. Behind her, she heard Rourke descend the stairs. Tears stinging her cheeks, Kat ran from the house and rushed to her car, and put it in gear.

She saw Rourke step onto the porch. Their eyes met. His fist hit the doorjamb, then he started toward the car at the same moment Kat floored the accelerator.

Liz laughed and opened the front door. Moments later, she had Kat by the arm and led her into the kitchen. "Sit," she ordered and shoved a box of tissues at Kat. "What happened?"

Unable to stop herself or censor her words, Kat told Liz every humiliating second of the story. "I've lost him," she sobbed. "I-I've lost Rourke to Clarissa!"

"Dry your eyes and stop wailing." Rising from her chair, Liz went to the sink, dampened a towel, and returned to Kat. "Here, wipe your face. Sometimes, my brother's a few fries short of a Happy Meal, but even at his dumbest he'd never get back with that bleached blonde. He can't stand her. I'll bet she showed up, stayed long enough to create trouble, and took off like a happy camper."

Kat shook her head. "Haven't you listened to a word I've said?" she asked, her voice rising with each word. "She'd been swimming. I smelled the chlorine. And Rourke was in the shower and when she left, he called out to her."

"Rourke isn't involved with Clarissa!"

"You weren't there. I saw—"

"I've listened to you, now you listen to me. Rourke was in a rage when I took the kids over. When I asked what was wrong, the first words out of his mouth were to ask if I'd seen you. When I told him not since this morning, he started ranting and raving about Clarissa and getting a restraining order. That does not sound like a lover to me."

Liz stood and pulled Kat from the chair. "Things will work out. I'm sure of it."

For the first time since she'd arrived, Kat looked at Liz and swallowed. Liz was the epitome of elegance, yet here she sat with her hair mussed and blouse misbuttoned. "Where's Carl?" Kat asked in a weak voice.

Liz grinned. "Upstairs waiting to continue celebrating our first child-free afternoon in six months."

"Oh, God, I was afraid you were going to say that," Kat moaned as she felt her face grow fiery hot. Kat couldn't believe she'd interrupted, much less that Liz left, her love nest.

"If I'd been thinking straight, I would have realized that—" Kat stopped mid-sentence unable to continue.

"Just out of curiosity, where've you been for the last hour and a half?"

Kat jumped to her feet. "At the movies and Baskin Robbins, drowning my sorrows in a killer banana split."

Shaking her head, Liz hugged Kat. "For once, take my advice. Call Rourke. Talk to him about what happened."

"Why? So I can hear more excuses?"

"My brother may be many things, including stupid where you're concerned, but he isn't a liar. Talk to him."

A tissue from the box on the counter shredded as she fiercely mopped her eyes. "I'll think about it tomorrow. Today I'm going to rent some movies and drown myself in a giant bowl of buttered popcorn."

Kat turned and headed for the door. As she pulled it closed, she heard Liz mutter, "That's my Kat. She faces all her problems head-on."

Rourke pulled into the driveway of 201 Maiden Lane and turned off the ignition. His knuckles tightened around his steering wheel. The car's air conditioner cooled, but didn't dry the rivers of sweat running down his face. He hadn't been this nervous when he'd asked a girl out for the first time at fourteen. But, then, his entire future hadn't rested on the answer.

His head dropped forward and rested on his hands. Between his actions and the "screech owl's," a bad situation had turned into a national incident. At least Liz had sufficiently forgiven him to give him a heads-up about Clarissa's lies.

Amazing how in less than twenty-four hours his perspective had changed. If necessary, he'd get down on bended knee and beg. Although, if Liz were to be believed begging wouldn't be necessary. It'd be like hitting a home run after two strikes.

"No time like the present." Rourke eased out of the car's bucket seat and headed for the front door. Hearing the television, he relaxed. She was home. He pressed the bell, then pressed again. By the third time, he wondered if he'd already struck out but didn't know it yet.

Shoulders hunched, he turned to leave. Hearing the deadbolt unlatch, he spun around and reined in his excitement. As the door opened, his smile dimmed. Tory's babysitter, Karen, stood in the doorway, cordless phone in her hand. Okay, if he couldn't see Kat, he'd talk to his one ally, Tory, and discover when he'd have his next chance at bat.

"Hi, Mr. Hawthorne. Come on in." Karen pressed the connect button. "I gotta go. Liz's brother's here."

Rourke followed Karen into the house and closed the door. "Why am I Mr. Hawthorne and my sister's Liz?"

"My mom said I had to use Mr. with anyone old enough to be my parent."

Rourke laughed. "Then you can safely call me Rourke. I'm only thirty-eight."

"*Really?* Gee, I thought you were younger than my mom."

Rourke stiffened. "Where's Tory?" Running feet pounded down the stairs. "Never mind."

"Uncle Rourke!" Tory squealed and jumped from the fourth step from the bottom.

As he caught Tory in a bear hug, her cast banged against the base of his head. Rourke consoled himself with the thought that given his recent behavior the whack could only have knocked some sense into it.

"See ya," Karen said, disappearing into the kitchen.

"She's gonna call her boyfriend. Mommy says Karen has three ears an' one of 'em is the phone."

Rourke chuckled and kissed Tory's forehead. "How're you doing, princess?"

"Okay. Mommy just left."

"Rats." He set her down and they walked into the living room. "How is she?"

Tory wrinkled her nose and shrugged her shoulders.

He knew he shouldn't ask, but would anyway. One more item on the list of errors. "Is she mad?" As tears welled up in Tory's eyes, Rourke sat and lifted her onto his lap. "It's okay, princess. You can tell me about yesterday," he murmured, wiping tears from her cheeks with his thumbs.

"She cried, an' muttered your name, an' ate bunches of popcorn, an' watched a movie."

A weak smile played at the corners of his mouth. No doubt the popcorn was loaded with butter. From childhood, Kat had drowned her grief, hurt and anger in food. She was damned lucky she never gained an ounce. Tory lifted her head and stared at him. Her intent gaze reminded him of Kat when she was trying to decide something important.

"What else, princess?"

"Well, the movie was kinda stupid and she watched two parts over and over and over and cried and cried."

The kid had a career in law—as a hostile witness. She answered exactly what was asked, nothing more or less. "Oh? What two parts?"

"This man says this lady should marry his brother. An' at the end this same man comes to her job, she works at the el, what's an el, Uncle Rourke?"

"An elevated railroad in Chicago. Then what happens in the movie?"

"Oh, yeah, he asks her to marry him with everyone watching."

While You Were Sleeping. It figured. *Come on, Rourke, think. There had to be a reason why she focused on those two parts, the two sappiest scenes in the movie. Then again, what'd he know?*

"Uncle Rourke? Why's Mommy sad?"

Rourke drew her against his chest and stroked her hair. "I said some things and now she's mad at me. But it was just a misunderstanding. I've hurt her feelings."

"Yeah, 'cause you love her."

"Right." His first break. His champion had returned. With Tory in his corner, he had the game in the bag. The two of them would work on Kat. Rourke sat beside Tory on the sofa, then squatted on the rug before her and took her hands in his. "You don't hate me, too?"

"Oh, no, Uncle Rourke." She smiled at him. "And Mommy doesn't neither." Tory paused, her eyes squinted in concentration. "Mommy said just remember never turn your back on someone, 'specially if he's Peter and he denies you three times before the rooster says 'cock-a-doodle-do'. What's that mean?"

"Never mind, princess." Rourke patted her hand and stood. "My name isn't Peter." He headed for the door. "Judas, maybe, but not Peter."

"Uncle Rourke?" Tory grabbed his hand. "Would you tell

Mommy you love her in front of everyone like the man in the movie?"

He swallowed hard. "I don't know, princess. I'm not sure I can do it." He momentarily closed his eyes. "Or even know how." He ruffled her hair. "Tell your mommy I stopped by, okay?"

"Uh-huh."

Rourke opened the door, then paused and looked back at Tory. "Sweetie, do you think thirty-eight is old?"

"Gee, Uncle Rourke, I don't know anyone *that* old."

Desperate and stupid were the two words that came to mind. He couldn't believe he'd stooped to begging a first-grader for reassurance and worse, not getting it.

"Right. See you later, princess." He walked slowly toward his car. Moments later he was on his way to his office. If he couldn't see Kat and try to work things out, then he might as well work. At least he hadn't denied her three times. Or had he? Rourke shook his head. It all depended on who was doing the counting.

By the time he pulled into his parking lot, he'd sorted through and discarded half a dozen approaches to woo Kat back to him.

As he slid out of his car, he notice two parked police cars. The uniformed officers stood talking to someone he couldn't see.

"May I help you, officers?" Rourke asked as he approached them. They separated and turned as a unit.

Rourke groaned. Leaning against the front fender of a Jaguar was a grinning Jason Barrington.

Dudley Doright's double pulled out his handcuffs. "You're under arrest, Mr. Hawthorne."

"I'm *what?*" Rourke's gaze jumped between the advancing officer and a snickering Jason. It figured. Labor Day weekend was turning out to be a labor of major proportions. He took a deep breath and faced Dudley's clone. "This is a product of a misunderstanding. I didn't mean—"

"To fall in love with my date," Jason interrupted. "But hey, after a short stint in jail, I'm willing to call it square."

Rourke's eyes narrowed. Something was off. Why hadn't he been Mirandized? "Officer what's—"

A photographer stepped forward. As soon as the cuffs were locked in place, he said, "Smile for the camera, Mr. Hawthorne."

Kat trudged back to her car. Twice, she'd come to Rourke's house, her pride and self-respect thrown to the wayside. What was it about this man and her love that made her lose all semblance of self-respect? "Come on, Kat, you haven't lost a thing. It isn't like this love is all that long standing."

Okay, today was Monday and she'd only admitted to herself that she loved him eight days ago. Well, kinda admitted, she corrected herself. Unfortunately, the eight days had consisted of a silent but declared war at work and a three day Labor Day weekend from hell.

She couldn't even see him to explain. First she'd run into Clarissa, tucked her tail between her legs, and ran. And now that she'd taken Liz's advice, she couldn't find him. She'd called his house, tried the office and had returned to his house again.

Lordy, she'd sunk to trying to jimmy the garage's side door lock. This torture could not continue.

Kat jerked open her car door. Time for Baskin Robbins!

Two hours later, Kat sat behind her steering wheel, stuffed full of double chocolate fudge and no closer to a solution. One thought had hammered at her through both banana splits; Rourke was with Clarissa. Her fingers twitched on the ignition key. Did she have the nerve? And supposing she did, what would she do if she found them together? Eat more triple banana splits, quit her job, and move out of the country.

As Kat turned the key, she spotted the message light of her car's cell phone blinking. Punching in the code, she heard Liz's voice quivering between laughter and hysteria. "Where are you? Rourke's in jail! Call me, ASAP!"

"Jail?" Jason! He must have pressed charges even after she'd called and begged him not to. A slow grin spread across Kat's face. She could handle jail, especially if she was the one to bail him out. Oh, yes, he'd do anything, even listen to her, to keep from being publicly humiliated.

Kat punched out Liz's number. The phone picked up halfway through its first ring.

"Where've you been for the past couple of hours? I've been going crazy trying to reach you!"

"Where's he being held?" Kat frowned. "Liz? Are you laughing?"

"Yup. I'm knee-slapping, tears-running laughing. Rourke's been thrown in the slammer."

"So your message said. Is Carl at the station bailing him out?"

"No way! Carl's sitting beside me howling like a fool."

Outrage filled her. Okay, so Rourke had refused to call Jason and apologize. That didn't give Carl the right to let Rourke cool his jets in jail. "Rourke's in jail and Carl, his attorney, hasn't gone down and bailed him out!"

"Yeah, well, Kat . . . Carl wants to know where you've been."

"Baskin Robbins. What's that have to do with Rourke being in jail?"

"Well, while you were indulging in your passion for ice-cream, Rourke's been indulging in theatrics." Liz snorted. "Turn on your radio. Any station'll do. I mean, it's the biggest story to hit the airwaves on a no-news day. You've got to get over to Independence Mall, now, and stop this before Rourke becomes the new poster child for Fruit Loops."

Kat tuned her radio to an all news channel, listened to the unfolding story, and began to laugh.

"This is Garrett Graham at CNN, Atlanta. Labor Day signifies the last day of summer. Sea, sunshine and romance. Well, folks, here's the story of one man who believes in love and he's caught the attention of all America. Rourke Hawthorne, a senior partner in the law firm Hawthorne and Vance in McLean, Virginia, has refused to leave jail all in the name of love. For more on this story, we go to Marian Carson at Independence Mall."

An attractive brunette stood in front of a mock jail. "As part of the MDA telethon, the Labor Day jail has become a tradition in these parts, especially the arrest of prominent citizens and high bail."

Leaning against the bars outside the jail, a man stood talking in hushed tones to one of the prisoners. Marian Carson turned and honed in on the two men like a heat-seeking missile. She held a microphone to the free man's face. "Mr. Barrington, you made the cover of this week's _M._ How's it feel to be hailed as a fashion trend-setter, bringing the marine-recruit look back in style?"

Jason raked a hand along his stubbly scalp and grinned. "Love it."

She laughed at Jason's wink. "The man behind the bars is Rourke Hawthorne. Mr. Barrington had you arrested, then posted your bail. You're a free man, Mr. Hawthorne. The cell door's unlocked, yet you refuse to leave. Why?"

Rourke faced the camera. "I'm not leaving here until the woman I love comes for me."

"That's it? She just has to show up and you'll leave?"

"She has to admit she loves me in spite of my being a Number Nine." Rourke plopped down in a metal chair next to the bars and folded his arms across his chest. The arrest had been bad enough, but all this media attention was driving him nuts. And what'd he have to show for it? Not a damned thing. Unless you counted humiliation that is.

With his luck, Liz "The Mouth of the South" was at the beach and unavailable to spread the word. That was the only explanation. Otherwise, Liz would have tracked Kat down and dragged her here, and worn a sandwich board around her neck inscribed with: Don't end up like my crazy brother. Call Dr. Liz Vance, Licensed Clinical Psychologist at 1-800-CRY-HELP.

Kat had been the one wild card. He'd hoped, prayed, she'd ignore her hatred of the spotlight and join him. But then he'd counted on his sister to give her the heads-up. As a back-up, he should have alerted Tory as soon as he'd been arrested. Instead, he'd decided to copy that damned movie scene and make a public declaration.

So far, all he had to show for his efforts was a camera and mike shoved in his face and Jason hovering around him with that shark smile of his.

"I can't believe you're doing this," Jason said out of the side of his mouth. "You, who hates publicity unless it's about a case." He snapped his fingers. "That's it. The press loves you and the story. Talk about free publicity for the firm."

Rourke shot him a glare. "Get a life," he growled, then grinned. "Rubbing it won't make it grow in faster."

Jason rubbed his almost hairless head. "Ah, but maybe it'll

grant me my three wishes: Kat appears, she doesn't inflict any more pain on my poor bod, and she disappears with you in tow."

"Yeah, right. This whole bit is out of character. What's in it for you?"

"Ensuring that a walking disaster, a woman who can cripple a man without trying, will be off the streets and in your bed."

Rourke returned the man's infectious grin. Shark or no, Jason was a nice guy. "I'm surprised you didn't file a formal complaint."

"Oh, because of this?" Jason stroked his slightly swollen jaw. "Hey, I figured you did me a favor. At the rate Kat was going, I wouldn't have made it through the night." All trace of a smile left his face. "Your insurance is paid up, isn't it?"

Rourke shook his head in amusement. "Yeah, it's paid up."

Jason glanced at his watch. "For a lady in love with you, she's sure into making her man suffer. Oops, spoke too soon." He nodded to a sable-haired woman walking toward them. "Don't blow it this time."

Rourke bolted to his feet and moved to the bars alongside the cell door. He grinned down at a crying and laughing Kat, then scowled at Marian Carson and her advancing cameraman. "Could you give us a few moments alone?"

"Just pretend I'm not here," she said and thrust her mike between them.

Rourke reached through the bars and took Kat's hands in his. "I know you think I'm Mr. Wrong. But I love you. Only you. I always have." Still holding onto her hands, he knelt before her. "Will you, Katherine Snow, do me the honor of becoming my wife?"

"Yes!"

Rourke stood and in two steps walked through the cell's open door. As it clanged shut behind him, he gathered Kat in his arms. "No backing out at the last minute." He lifted his gaze and scanned the assembled crowd of shoppers and reporters. "I have witnesses."

"Seal it with a kiss!" Jason called out.

Rourke ignored Kat's initial tension. "We're the stuff dreams are made of," he whispered against her lips just before he covered them in a kiss that left the crowd cheering.